BOOK I

JOHN ROYAL WARREN
&
VIENNA NICOLE

OCTOBER LEAF PRESS

ISBN 979-8-9989315-0-5

Edited & Designed by Vienna Nicole & John Royal Warren
Cover Photo by Cottonbro Studio | www.cotton.film | instagram/cottonbro
Title Typography/Graphic Design by John Royal Warren

Library of Congress Control Number: 2025912960

Publisher's Cataloging Data
Warren, John Royal. Nicole, Vienna
The Dread Legacies: Victoria Frankenstein / October Leaf Press.—1st Edition

ISBN 979-8-9989315-0-5 (trade pbk.)
ISBN 979-8-9989315-1-2 (e-book)
ISBN 979-8-9989315-2-9 (hardcover)
ISBN 979-8-9989315-3-6 (variant art hardcover)
1. Fiction—Horror. 2. Thriller. First Edition
DDC: 813.6

October Leaf Press, 725 N Bingham Ave, Somerton, AZ 85350

Find the playlist on Spotify and Youtube

"The Dread Legacies Playlist"

"Ultraviolet" **Freya Ridings**

"Borders" **Kalandra**

"For whom the fires burn(winterscape remix) **PHILDEL**

"The Fruits" **Paris Paloma**

"1816 The Year Without A Summer" **Rasputina**

"So Human Of You" **Shireen**

"Carrion Comfort" **aeseaes**

"Light that match" **Down Like Silver**

"Don't Let Me Go" **RAIGN**

"Big Houses" **Squalloscope**

"Claude's Girl" **Marika Hackman**

"Moment" **Roses & Revolutions**

"Premonitions" **Vaults**

"Rule #9 – child of the stars" **Fish in a Birdcage**

"Brave new world" **Kalandra**

"Conscious" **BROODS**

"Darkness Inside" **Astyria**

"Burn" **Astyria**

"Throne" **Saint Mesa**

"Lie alone" **Blanco White**

"As It Was" **Hozier**

TABLE OF CONTENTS

These warnings are only found here.
There are no warnings at the start of chapters.

CONTENT WARNING:
This content contains mature situations, violence, and what some may consider gore and inappropriate for children.
Discretion is advised.

TRIGGER WARNING:
Some of these chapters contain depictions of violence, death, child death and child sexual assault that may be upsetting for some readers.
Discretion is strongly advised.

This Book Is Dedicated To:

Our sisters, to our mothers, to our Grandmothers.
To those who still dream,
and to all those who have stopped.
And to our Persephone,
You are the kindness we always wanted in this world.
You are our legacy.

Victoria
Frankenstein

Chapter 1

Victoria Frankenstein

The Frankenstein name was one of opulence and whispered envy, as excess set them apart from even the highest royal courts. Amid November's autumn, in the year of 1805, while the high society of England reveled in sumptuous balls, exquisite theaters, and endless libations, the Mount Olympus specter of the Frankenstein lineage had become a ghost story. They wield a status that their wealth provides. Voices shudder when they rumor the Frankenstein name in whispers to both the wives and their title holding husbands. The rumor mill of wealthy families, who are safe to roam the corridors within their warm manors and city homes. The young grow plump with meals their mothers never cook for them, and they shop for new attire regularly to wear the finest clothes that they can afford a tailor to seam for them. It cannot be denied that these people are living comfortably while enjoying the splendors of the world. With loyal subjects to handle mundane everyday tasks, it frees up their time to find leisure, to enjoy the arts, to taste the abundance of food served freely, and to actively attend parties and weddings. Yet in this crowd of crystal cups and silk dresses, there is no Frankenstein. Nor are they found in quiet corners or private dinners. Not within the lecture halls or university classrooms. England has not seen a Frankenstein amidst its streets in eighteen years.

Far from society in the southwest of Germany, bordering France, the Frankenstein castle resides. A Schloss castle with seven stories looms mountainous on a rock in the middle of a massive lake. Complete with flying buttresses, countless towers, domes, and wings. A truly visionary love letter to Gothic architecture. A mighty landmark for the Frankenstein's symbol of status. Thick forest and wild mountain ranges lay on the opposite side of the lake from the castle, resembling an oil painting of yellows and hazel hues where the green of spring is dying.

As the evening makes its comfortable arrival, the castle lives silently with emptiness. Without a soul to see the setting sun pass through its hundreds of windows. No maids, no cooks, and no loyal servants have roamed these halls in some weeks, and the quiet that rests on the walls is one shrouded in mourning. An abandoned graveyard of bouquets can be found in the ballroom. Their dried-up and withered corpses are gone unloved. Piles of melted candles can be seen crowding the corners of a few rooms. The stillness of time throughout the castle, with black fabric draped across portraits, mirrors, and scattered furniture, has left nothing more than the solemn silence of a once illustrious home.

As the dawn is snuffed out by a starless night sky, a woman of forty-four with black hair sleeps peacefully against a frost-smudged windowpane. She rests on an icy cushioned window nook. Her fair, almost ageless face relaxes lightly, as if sheltered by dreams rather than the chill that crept in. Victoria Frankenstein wakes. Her deep contemplative eyes open to survey her castle grounds in the throes of night. For a moment, she is still, and all is calm. Reflecting in her eyes is a crackle of lightning that scrapes across smoky black clouds. An electrical storm is rising. She then brings her legs off the nook and marches with a measured haste. She steps through corridors adorned with hanging oil lamps that are not lit, paired with ornate patterns of callous shadows from floor to ceiling. "In solitude," she murmurs to herself, not without a hint of irony, "there is a clarity of thought few can claim." Her tone was not of resignation but of burning resolve. She journeys to the other side of the castle. Dressed not in the customary fall gown but in finely tailored dark trousers, a crisp tweed vest, and a simple long cotton coat. This outfit serves as her statement to rebel against a world stifled by convention. Victoria moves with her dark hair loosely wafting behind her. Her measured steps lead her through corridors lined with dormant oil lamps and shadowy arches, each footfall echoing before reaching the master bedroom. What is meant to be a bedroom doubles as a library where each wall is covered up by dark wood bookshelves; each one filled with red leather bound journals in row after row. Each journal is guaranteed to be filled with her documentation and notes.

There is a window that reaches from floor to ceiling, climbing a precise twenty-five feet. Aggressively she draws the curtains back on it. Living beside the window is a writing desk. The loyal tools of her workshop are loose parchment paper, a quill and ink, and a loop-handle candlestick holder, all neatly prepared on top of her desk. Before she can light the candle, a silent tide of light splashes the drafty room in a blink. A light explodes to life on the matchstick she uses to ignite the desk's candle. Adjusting the quill between her fingers, she eagerly sits down to a blank sheet of paper. In a moment she ponders how there is a razor judgment for a woman who has such wealth and still makes no allegiances with the men who wish to grow their fortunes larger. To add to her position, she is alone in her ancestral home, which leaves many to speculate suspicions especially in high society. "Hmm... Then what a rare and fortunate position I must be in," she thinks, "a rare case of one such woman. To be alone with her thoughts and allowed to think unhindered. With the wealth to make actions of her ideas. Monstrous ideas. Committed as any man, I am, only because I live as... the other."

She starts writing with her ink-dipped quill in the weak glow of dying candlelight. She sits at her desk assertively, writing every word with self-appointed discipline. Furthermore, she can smell stale musk when wetting the hemp parchment paper with every line of ink. Her black wavy hair falls to one side, resting on a shoulder. The music of rain hitting the glass of her windows can be heard coinciding with the quiet scratching sound her quill makes when writing. She writes:

"I, Victoria Frankenstein, on this the year 1800 and the 5th. November the 5th, believe it is of the upmost importance to journal additional details before I conduct my experiment in any case of misfortune throughout. I have, for twenty-two years, researched rare cases of a disease. From these cases I have taken blood from men and women for further studies. The samples' origins:

Egypt, in the year 1783. A man with this disease was mummified. The disease allowed him to survive thousands of years in dormancy as long as his organs remained removed from his body. He was the most powerful of all cases I have ever encountered. His blood, immortal. I expand on this case in further detail in my journal labeled 'King of the Dead.'

Point Pleasant, the Americas, in the year 1784.

This case is still shrouded in grand mystery. Blood was obtained from a massive creature that was black and winged with red eyes. I have documented this encounter in further detail in my journal labeled 'Point Pleasant.'

Gevaudan, France, the year 1785.

A woman who was relieved of ailments or any harm by her disease also would suffer a frontal lobe takeover while her body underwent a flooding of hormones of both estrogen and testosterone and adrenaline in the night of full moons. I expand on this case in my journal labeled 'Beast of Gevaudan.'

Lastly, I have obtained blood from my love of 19 years, Voivode. He is a man truly cursed with every purposeful enrichment of the phrase. There are a tremendous number of similarities his version of this disease shares with a variety of illnesses. His pale complexion could define him as having the white plague, but he shares no other symptom and defies the end result of the disease, which is death. A sensitivity to sunlight is a common connection to rabies. In Voivode's case it is more than a hindrance; it whittles his body, destroys his flesh, and rumples him into a charred living carcass. Porphyria causes a hypersensitivity to light as well but never to a damaging extreme such as he experiences. There must be an ingestion of blood if he is ever to be damaged by the sun in order to recover; therefore, an absence of the need for blood is his general everyday living. In spite of these factors, Voivode is immortal. I expand further on his case in my journals, "The Son of the Dragon." All four cases are like any disease with damning drawbacks, but in all four cases there is a profoundly rare healing factor that I hope and dream I can enable in dead human tissue. I am far from understanding how this blood and disease truly function and if there is any such way to manipulate them, but if I could, it would mean an advancement in medicine that would give the recently deceased a second chance at life. A cure for child illnesses, possibly those such as measles. The potential is there for bettering the well-being of all human life. There is no fathom to the limitless progress humanity can propel to. The death of the young who potentially hold answers and keys to creating a utopian future can be given a second chance to gift us with their imagination. Less creativity and love will be lost so we all can rise higher as the human collective. No mother will have to lose their child again. Evidently no child will have to lose their mother to have life. My motivation overflows with a terrible exuberance in my every waking day. To see success in a one-in-a-trillion probability would mean more than changing the world, more than the advancements of medicine, and more than a bright and bold future. In truth, what is most important to me is that it would mean I would get back the heart I lost in this world. The love in me this world extinguished.

It is with tremendous shame and dismay that I must disclose a wretched confession. In the past day I have grave-robbed the body of a Mathys Holl, who passed in the last week. He met his demise in an accident as he came to collapse under a windmill's water wheel. He suffered cranial damage in the back and top of his skull, destroying his brain. I transplanted into him a brain and eyes. I have surgically implanted 4 electricity conduits into the body. Two on either side of the torso. I have also combined the blood of all four previously mentioned cases. The result was a biological luminescence that I believe is two chemicals that I have known to be common in sea life, was present in two separate collections of blood. With only enough to fill two vials after mixing. I will be injecting one full vial into the body while it lies in a vat of water. Soon after, I will engage an electrical current from a battery that will be connected to the four electricity conduits in the torso. Allowing for electricity to course through the body.

To further explain, in the year 1796 I began funding the experiments of Alessandro Volta. He is an Italian physicist that was working to invent a machine that will produce electricity over a long period of time, steadily. I take no credit for his work, having only been present for his experiments eight or so visits in under ten years. When he finally invented the voltaic pile in the year 1799, we worked together in secret to create a version of the voltaic pile that produced 100-200 watts instead of 1-2 watts, which is what his invention initially supplied. We eventually became successful, and I possess such a machine that I have named "The Box." I will use it to produce a steady current of electricity into the body through the electricity conduits in the torso over the course of six hours. The hope is that the end result will be that the aforementioned disease in the combined vials of blood will take hold of the cells while they are surging with a steady current of electricity. Allowing for the cells to adopt the disease's regenerative effects and heal the dead cells back to life. If there are no problematic occurrences and I am without harm, I shall return to record my findings. This concludes my record."

Placing the quill beside the ink jar, Victoria turns to get up from the desk, but halfway up she stops herself and a hurt curried on the love of her heart now runs through her, drenching her eyes in longing. Gently, she sits back down. Her hand resting on the desk calmly drifts over to pick up the quill once again. Her eyes gloss with sentiment as the point of the quill starts a new page. She writes, "I said goodbye to my love today. I watched from my windows as his charcoal black horses took his carriage through the castle gates. I stared with painful concentration, hoping I could somehow see through the charter's black-painted windows and maybe catch a glimpse of him once more. I watched him leave; though I am not unfamiliar with the sight, it does not make it any less difficult. I stayed long after he was gone when the sun peeked over the horizon. I looked on till I fell asleep against the pane."

The wind is whispering through the high windows as Victoria allows herself a moment of vulnerable introspection before resuming her resolute penmanship. Every diligent stroke of her quill is a confession of the heart. Under the blinding pulse of lightning flashes, she is not distracted. "His travels will take him far from me. Though it is nothing I wouldn't expect, for the legacy he is building is far greater than any fictional giant. I also think about my legacy. I wonder what the world will write of me 200 years from now. I know they will tell of how I advanced mankind with such unmatched haste. Children will idolize me as the hero they strive to someday be. I will lie here in my bed tonight, and I will not cry for what I have lost! I will not cry for the absence of my love. My father, the glorious man that he was, always said, "Death follows Frankensteins," so I say let him follow, for I will never slow, I will never halt. Every inch of my being, until my last breath, will constantly strive to fulfill my dreams. I will get back to my heaven. I will get back my life. As I doze off, I will be imagining what history will write of me, as someday they will erect a monument in my likeness as a memorial of my achievements. Doctor Victoria Frankenstein. The angel of life. I dream... so often it becomes a wool over my eyes. A facade of mountains built with delusions of grandeur that, when it fades, a dull, colorless perspective remains. The tightening of a noose can be felt then around my neck, and I shed stinging, forced tears. I dream. And I dream, because I carry with me a moratorium. Inside it holds the tomb of my mother, whom I have never known, for she passed shortly after I was born. The child I lost while still in my womb. The tomb of my father, who perished in Egypt in the winter of the year 1783. A lifetime of lovers who came years before my current companion, Voivode, are all but corpses now. I dream because they cannot. I dream because if they could still be here, they would want me to dream. For them I keep my dreams protected in a chamber I keep near my heart. Impenetrable and invulnerable to corruption and never in need of the sustenance of glory or ego. It was my grief of being followed by loss that I desired to spite death itself. The beauty of my memories has tarnished; therefore, the moral boundaries I have crossed to see the happiest part of my life returned to me mustn't be to no avail. This will be a home again."

Victoria gets up from her desk to then dress down. She collects the recently written pages and closes them inside a red leather-bound journal, putting a flattened white lotus flower in the back of the pages before closing it. Only wearing her undergarments, she walks with haste across the castle to the bergfried. Defined as the tallest tower in the castle and usually reserved to be constructed in the middle of an architecture, it is found instead at the back of the Frankenstein castle.

She enters a chamber designed to be mercilessly clean. Four basins waited against the wall. She methodically works from fingertip to elbow, scrubbing and rinsing twice until the skin stings and the water runs grey with yesterday's oils.

She dresses with economical ceremony. A second set of tailored undergarments cut like a man's, then heavy rubber overalls. Over that she drew a long white coat. Doctor's lines, subtly altered to the slope of her shoulders. A hair cover snaps into place, a surgical mask hides the lower plane of her face, and she slides black rubber gloves up past her elbows until only whiteness and the small dark oval of her eyes remain.

Journal tucked beneath her arm, she passes through the outer door, each step calculated as if leaving behind herself and stepping into her work.

The large body of a corpse lies under a white sheet on a metal table that is hanging off the ground by five feet. In the darkness, light flashes from the heedless dancing of lightning, proceeded by thunder, sending a tremble through the Frankenstein castle. The strobes of light fill the room until Victoria enters, and she begins to flip switches on a board that is in direct control of an electrical source that brings to life bulbs beaming with illumination in every corner of the room's darkness. The technology in this room alone isn't just made up of prototypes but the newest inventions from all over the world that only one with the means to find them and the wealth to obtain them could have. This laboratory mirrors the previous sanitary room with the scale expanded. There is a frightening coldness to the white cleanliness of the floors and walls. Alarming even, to see a room devoid of artistry and expression. With clear surfaces and finely cut edges, like stepping out of time into a room that is abundantly designed for clean medical treatment, further setting it out of place.

Victoria takes every step with purpose as well as every movement of her hands, led by a predetermined plan. Operating with a choreography practiced in the playground of her thoughts a thousand times over. She primes the syringe until it hums with a milky blue light, a small captive dawn in glass. Behind her, the Box wakes with a dry, electric crackle like distant ice shifting.

Beneath the iron slab where the massive shape of the man lies is a basin deep enough to swallow the table whole. Victoria moves with a choreography. Soon her fingers find the faucet and twist. The pipes moan as the tub fills. She cuts the flow, then eases the table down until metal meets water with a dull, obedient groan.

Leaning over the pool, she peels the sheet back, pausing to stare at them. She lays the cloth back over him but does not hurry. Her pause is not mercy so much as an appraisal, a final reading of the man she will make.

Outside, the storm begins its sermon. Lightning knives the sky; thunder answers like a dropped anvil. Each flash etches the ceiling window; each boom makes the lab feel smaller. Victoria looks up once, then covers the face completely.

She speaks to herself aloud while staring out the window at the ceiling, "Like the mysteries of what electricity is, so is the uncertainty or truth to the extent to which we can control life and death. We can see it, make use of it, feel storms of the heart, and try to capture it in words. But there is no maker of magic or nature. We do, in action, to undo its mysteries and make less fear of the unknown."

Through the castle gates, across the limestone bridge, and down a twisty road, there reside the gates of an old medieval Bavarian town down the hill. Little rain from the storm has happened upon its ensemble of colorful half-timbered houses. The autumn breeze carries bright foliage through the winding narrow alleys. The townspeople are made up of women wearing high-waist gowns with long muslin skirts and men in dim or dark-colored breeches, with some in long, loose, and coarse overcoats and others in tweed vests and jackets. They come out of their homes and crowd the twisty cobblestone streets. The lightning's voltage can be heard coming from the thunderstorm over the Frankenstein castle. Between every explosion of thunder a wave of fear courses through the towns people resulting in shutters slamming shut on the flowers that pour over window boxes, while the crowd that is growing outside collectively gasp and clutch their chests. The town is wrought with hanging street signs that start to violently sway with unwanted screeches of iron.

He pushes out of the press of bodies like a knuckle through cloth. Wet lederhosen clinging to his thighs, leather boots sluicing mud with each step. Sweat plasters his hair to a forehead set in a scowl that looks carved. In one hand he bears a torch, its sputtering flame a stubborn heart against the bustling winds.

Moving through the crowd, he raises the light high. His voice cuts the wind, sharp, sudden, and raw. Sending a jagged sound that accosts people at their spine. Heads turn. Silence thinning to a wire. The torch's glow lights up faces and fear as he screams, "The devil is in our community! Victoria Frankenstein commits acts of heresy as we all stand by, we allow that heretical perversity to grow in the land of our lord. Exodus 22:18: Thou shalt not suffer a witch to live! She is the last of her lineage. She is alone inside the Frankenstein castle! For years she has been behind those walls, dwelling, hiding a secrecy of her life. Under the guidance and protection of God I have suspected her of WITCHCRAFT! She must be persecuted!" his final words hoarse with venom. A wave of gasps passes over the townsfolk.

"Turn away not now, for the works of evil are at hand! Turn away not and see before you now the proof! See before you with your eyes the truth. If Victoria is left unimpeded, who knows how strong her companionship with the devil will get? It is up to us to destroy her evil and the evil of her allegiance with the devil!"

An older man with a gray, fretted beard screams from the back of the crowd, "What acts of heresy do you submit Victoria has done?"

The town crier swings his lanky body around with his torch and screams back without hesitation, "We have all borne witness to the carriage, the one that blends in the darkness of night. The Devil himself comes to the witch, Frankenstein, to bestow his bidding onto her. He has finally instructed her to do the most unspeakable thing! She grave-robbed the body of Mathys Holl! His funeral was not but six days ago! I had come in from fishing last midnight to see her hauling his body. Tonight I dug up his grave, and my suspicions were confirmed. There lies no man, but an empty coffin! These eyes," he drives his pointer finger into the center of his chest aggressively, "my eyes... are of the son of a witch hunter, a child of God. My bloodline can be followed back to that of a crusader! There is no lie I wish to tell."

He points to a gaunt young woman with similar features to his own. "That is my sister." Then he points to a rigid-looking man with wrinkles that betray his age. "And my brother!" He continues to gesture to various people in the crowd. "My family founded this town generations ago, leading us all into God's gentle light." His brows furrow as he looks onward. "That storm lay over top her castle because it is with her that God is angered, and we must rise now, lest we all perish to a witch's will."

• • • •

IN THE LABORATORY VICTORIA drives the needle of a syringe between the corpse's ribs, and the baby blue starlight glow inside of it disappears. She reaches over, placing the syringe in a nearby copper pan, while the rest of her observes like gunpowder is being mixed, cautious of a dangerous reaction. There is one snake-like cable connected to "The Box." She drags it over. Clamps four loose wires at the end of the cable to each of the four conduits in the corpse's torso.

Four chains are attached to each corner of the iron slab and disappear upward into the ceiling, part of a pulley that could lift the whole table. The hoist is bolted where the only skylight framed the storm.

When Victoria clamps The Box's cable to the four conduits in the body, a new current finds its path. Near the ceiling, where the chain meets the hoist, iron rises on end as if prickled by static, and tiny shards and filings prick the air.

In the town below, a commotion brews where it took little effort for most of the townspeople to be persuaded to persecute Victoria. Torches ignite in a red glow as a group of them gather, wielding pitchforks on their march out of town. Together they ascend the twisty road and across the limestone bridge to the Frankenstein castle under an icy downpour. The mob reaches the castle and attempts to set it ablaze. They find it difficult in the torrent of rain but continue to try as a group of men break off to use nearby lumber as a battering ram on the castle doors.

Victoria cannot hear the banging because of the deafening humming sound that "The Box" is making, combined with the thunder tearing through the night.

The townspeople of Mill Valley learn, slowly and furiously, that brute force will not undo the iron and oak of the doors. Rain scours their torches and made fire a joke. Frustration sharpens into invention. Lumber is dragged like a new limb, fitted into a crude ramp, and hauled against the slick flank of the castle wall where a window resides high and out of reach. Men swear and slip. One, smaller and wiry as a ferret, keeps finding purchase where others cannot. He climbs with the hunger of someone who has nothing left to lose.

In his fist a palm-sized stone becomes a hammer. When he reaches the top, he pummels the window until the glass surrenders. Rain and shards go falling. For a beat he simply stands there. Soaked, shaking, and ridiculous with triumph, he slings the ramp through the jagged hole and drops down into the warmth of the hall. His boggling eyes taking in grandeur unfamiliar to him.

Soon the double doors tear open. The mob pours in, carrying the damp, sputtering teeth of their torches. They fan through the rooms with animal hunger, ripping down curtains and upending chairs, pressing piles of fabric and broken wood to the cold stone. Setting raging fires throughout. A cluster of men aim for the portrait of Victoria by the entrance, an affront, they say, to their fury. But it hangs stubbornly between stone pillars, twenty feet out of reach. They test ropes that fail and then simply throw their torches at it. Still her portrait holds as strong and secure as Victoria herself. Frustration turns on itself, and they abandon the attempt, taking their indignation and destruction deeper into the castle.

• • • •

INSIDE OF THE LABORATORY, Victoria stands beside "The Box" and watches a rod that protrudes from the top of The Box's housing. The rod is 3 feet long with a sphere at the end. Here in this moment as she waits patiently beside The Box, gripping her journal on one side of her, she slowly peers over her laboratory from one side to the other, stopping on the giant corpse of a man that is hoisted in a tub. Here, she recognizes doubt in her ethics. After a moment of self-reflection, she speaks passionately aloud, "Be my choice wrong or with greater or harsher judgment than that of 350 years of illogical and unethical torture and murder of all who perished under persecution of witchcraft? The world is covered in homes where the dead spirits stage life scorched by fires used to burn those at the stake. Weary of innocent souls drained from the beauty of time. If I am to be found immoral, then my immorality sits at the distance of the moon from that of the practices of slavery, for there is no closeness in comparison. It is of the greatest immorality to say, 'Give me your life, agreed, or I shall take it by force, and with your life in my hands, I care not how it is fumbled or crushed; only that you provide your indentured servitude, with suffering or not, till you can not be used to provide anymore.' My tampering of dead flesh and reanimation brings no pain, creates no harm, and cowers in comparison to the monstrously rudimentary practices of medicine, physicians, and hospitals alike." She screams, "Listen to me now! If the forces at work truly disagree with my experiments, may Zeus himself ride down on bolts of lightning to punish me!"

It's then that she sees static electricity form around the sphere. Static freckles. Instinct snaps her hand to the lever, and she flips it, an execution of fate.

The cable took the charge with a hungry hiss. For a sliver of time she traces the current's journey and watches a pale serpent uncoiling through copper, through the conduits, then spilling into the water with a silver scream. The charge did not die there. It slithers up the chains, slick and deliberate.

Her eyes climb with it and hit the ceiling where the hoist, made of a fine steel, is fastened. A cold, alarming sense runs through Victoria that a mistake has escaped her, and there is a dangerous precedent in her oversight. The consequences... are going to be unavoidable. They will bite back. The window above flares, a light so clean it strips color from the bulbs and bleaches the room to new edges. Every hair along her arms bristles upright. The vibration of metals sings. Trays and syringes tugging to be free of gravity, hovering, spitting blue and white sparks that stitch the air. The laboratory stilled beneath a thunder that hadn't yet arrived. A suspended second before catastrophe. Her mind, her Frankenstein mind, for as quick as it moves, is made to feel the world waiting for what was on the other side of her choices. Her mistakes.

• • • •

MILLIONS OF MILES AWAY… in the darkness, empty space of unimaginable size is home to a void outside of our galaxy. In the maddening orchestra of stars, a violent collision of a dwarf planet and a moon takes place. It is catastrophic devastation in the wake of these two celestial juggernauts colliding. The decomposition of organic matter releases blasts. The absolute annihilation sparks the conception of an energy. This energy makes a cosmic ray that is shot out into space as it is projected by a devastating shock wave the collision creates. This high-energy particle travels at super speed through space. It enters our galaxy. Eventually it enters our solar system.

Unbeknownst to Victoria, she is about to experience a phenomenon and be the only person to see up close a lightning strike caused by an impossible particle. A cosmic ray is traveling from extragalactic reaches of space, and it carries with it levels greater than exa-electron volts, which is measured to be millions of times more energy than anything that humans can produce on earth. It enters the atmosphere and intertwines with a lightning bolt.

In milliseconds that lightning bolt breaks through the window in the ceiling and rides down the chain hoist. It travels through the metal table, the corpse, the water, and into the cable.

The large voltaic pile drinks the electrical current in and then, overwhelmed, betrays its hunger. With a white flash that sears the edges of vision and a sound like a cannon split in two, the box detonates, not a tidy burst but a wild unspooling of flame and wire. Electricity lancing the air in jagged tongues. Heat hammers the room. Victoria is thrown as if struck by invisible tides, her body slamming the floor in a stunned arc. Darkness folds over her eyelids briefly, with the strength of strong sedatives, while the lab convulses around the epicenter of its own making.

Alarmingly, she awakens, breathing in smoke. Heat pressing at her ribs. The world tastes of ember. She inhales once, and the smoke steals the breath back, coughing fury into her throat. Her hands grab at her ruined lab. Surfaces gone molten in places, instruments shattered and glittering in millions of pieces.

Her fingers found glass and grit, then the familiar leather of her journal, warm and singed at the edges. She clutches it to her chest as if it were her heart almost lost to the disaster. Beyond the swirl of ash she could just make out her experiment, half-buried under the collapsed roof and ruined wiring. A pulse of helplessness hit her, for she knows that to cross that inferno now would be to trade everything for nothing. Time, the cruelest accomplice, accelerated. The flames climb with a greedy intelligence, consuming more and more. There was no time. She tried to imagine a way back, a path of wet cloths and courage, but the heat rose fast enough to blister thought. She forces herself up, each painful movement siphoning a bit more of her strength. The lab door lay open through the smoke. As the fire tyrannically burns to temperatures she cannot grapple with, she instinctively moves toward the door, boots wincing over scattered ash. At the threshold she pauses, one hand on the frame, the journal pressed to her breast, feeling the tug of everything left inside. All her work, a lifetime's quiet ambition to save those who are in the dark.

For a breath that stretched like a held note, she balances on the knife-edge, the world narrowing to the choice she has to make. There is no other way to save her experiment and survive. She turns back, dropping her shoulders as she begins to cry. "Forgive me!" She yells into the fire and smoke, "Forgive me!" She yells through the tears, "Forgive me!" She yells with heartbreak riding on the trembling decibels of her words.

She runs through the halls of her castle without questioning how the fires reached the other wings. An ever-unraveling disappointment of failure takes hold of her as she navigates to escape the burning castle.

She ponders, "Is this where God has disowned me? Has he been here all along, and I ignored the presence he took so I may foolishly keep the dead I could not let go? Here I voyage from my deeds without God. My punishments could be as severe as hearing only noise in the grace of music, and I would wallow, knowing I deserved it."

Her sorrowing makes her fall ill as she continues onward down flights of stairs. She continues in thought, "An arrow was pulled back, and with my guiding hand it was shot. Shot with good intention and confidence in its success, but still only just the one arrow. Only one opportunity to hit the target. The brain—it was a person; there was a life there. Memories no one can have. Now, they never will. The days where there was rain instead of sun and the lungs were filled with petrichor. The warm meals with family, never a night alone or without a full stomach. The warming touch of sunlight on the eyes in spring."

She pauses to weep, grabbing on to a door frame to hold her from falling while gripping her journal to her chest. She weeps uncontrollably as though she has never wept. As though she were attending a funeral.

She presses forward as the flames follow her and push her out into the gardens. She keeps going, stumbling minimally as she continues in her provoked thoughts, "Burden me! I wanted it! I wished for it and sought it out. Burden me with something to love. A child to give love and a purpose to never tire of. "Burden me," I asked, I demanded. "I am strong enough," I said. Remove my hand, burn me with frost, drown me in fire, and I will show you the meaning of loving and to love. Burden me. I will never tire. Death follows Frankensteins."

Now standing at the back of the castle gardens, she watches as all the castle windows spill over with flames.

"Is this God?" She ponders, "Is he ashamed? I ask. Then he provided, and I could not live up to my self-anointed merit? Or was my oversight so horrendously epochal that no act of divine punishment was needed? Or was the hand that sows a puppeteer to my decisions?"

The fire has grown to be so big that the heat from the flames is too much for Victoria that even standing at the back of the gardens is unbearable.

Victoria takes to a stairwell that leads to a pier. She dashes to a rowboat at the end of the pier and climbs aboard frantically, setting her journal down in the boat and rowing out onto the lake. She cries as she rows, watching her ancestral castle burn down. A 300-year-old castle that took 200 years to build and only one Victoria Frankenstein to burn down.

As she reaches the middle of the lake, she sees something escape the flames and emerge onto a balcony under a row of flying buttresses on the seventh story of the wing next to the laboratory. She stops rowing and stands in the boat. There is a massive figure silhouetted by the fires. She pauses in awe before celebrating accomplishment with a gasp and a jump.

"Alive? He's... alive!"

But her celebration is short-lived when a few men arrive on the balcony. Victoria watches in confusion from the middle of the lake as the men proceed to attack her experiment mercilessly. Victoria is filled with horror already, as she can only stand and watch when the tides turn. A silence smothers the world as the rain recedes and the clatter of thunder takes a pause when Victoria's creation explodes with power in retaliation, tearing five men apart.

Her palm impulsively reaches out before her in shock. Her fingers are stretched apart, and she can see her hand and arm silhouetted by the fire that engulfs her castle. Slivers of light can be seen emitting from the body of her massive creation... like a monster. The same mysterious light can barely be seen glowing from its eyes. A flood of questions and curiosities whirl like the winds in a tornado in Victoria's mind.

In the moments as she watches, she asks herself, "Have I birthed a titan so unstoppable?" Victoria tries to decipher what she can of her creation from its movement in the dark. She homes in on some of those thoughts in the hurricane of her mind. "I imagine there is no world that finds itself safe from a creation such as this. 100 feet tall, immeasurable strength, and no limits to what more they are capable of. With the blood of all four subjects that I manipulated in an attempt to remove or reduce the drawbacks of the disease and combine them in a single body, there are 4 truths I foresee of my creation's biology. One, there is no wound it cannot heal from, as their cells regenerate as fast as a breath. Two, unbridled strength with muscle fibers that imitate the density of steel. Three, mutation. There is not enough I could record in my years of research to understand why different individuals reacted in a unique way to the disease. But there was a pattern, and in three cases they had a mutation that made them deadlier. Four, it will be immune to illness, disease, starvation, and mortal wounds. It is immortal. I grow sicker within my bowels and breathing at the sheer imagining of my own creation arriving before me. What misery I imbued on it. Is there pain it feels? Is pain a sense for it? How much pain have I caused it? Whatever the motivation may be, I cannot conceive that our meeting will be without a shared resemblance to the effortless removal of a man's entrails and dismantling of the human form in one smooth swinging motion. How dare I ask only now? Was I wrong? How beautiful a creature, to curse the world like a form of arts opposite, plant a gaze on horror that unsettles the soul but inflicts a towering fear to turn away. Like soldiers at war, two children in a uniform placed on the battlefield to look each other in the eyes. Deterring their eyes from the other could mean an opponent's opportunity to strike the killing blow of a blade entering the heart. They fear to turn away lest doom come for them. So is the fear my creation inflicts. I can feel... the summer of my life begin to drain from my hair; a woman of forty-four sees more in the lessening of ability than that of growing ambition. There now lies among the lost, one's fearlessness to endure."

Panic rises in her as more townspeople arrive to meet the horrors of her creation's rampage. She can feel that chamber near her heart that holds her dreams being crushed. The walls that hold up her dreamer's soul were before now unbowed and impossible to abandon. Now, they beckon to forfeit as those walls begin to crumble and collapse. Single-handed gore and bloodshed like she's never seen is spread across the balcony. She sinks into an ocean of emotions, disappearing further into a darkness that light and air fear from as she drowns in despair. There is no breath she could take that could breathe life back into her broken dreams.

Lightning strikes, bursting in the sky like an orchestra for nature, reaching crescendos whenever the townspeople are split up the middle and cut down by Victoria's creation. From the middle of the lake, she stands in her rowboat under the dark of night while being pelted by the rain, looking on with terror into the flames. She feels the death of a part of her within but also the birth of an unexplored era. The birth of dread.

Chapter 2

Winter of 1816

Near the North Pole, the winter wind throws snow in sheets that shiver like a congregation of pale ghosts. Wave after wave of flurry erases and rewrites the world. The horizon, existent but unattainable. Against an eight-mile-an-hour wind, a lone silhouette trudges, bundled in layers of sodden furs and wool, goggles obscured in frost. Each step is a small argument with the tundra.

They halt with a kind of suddenness. Through the sleet a shadow looms, not terrain, but a grand structure. It's a ship. A brilliant ship protruding out of the ice like a fossilized leviathan. Obscene against the white, a Tudor carrack of Italian make, more than five centuries old, lay embalmed in the glacier's grip.

They start running to it, boots scabbed with frozen spray, and find a ladder hewn against the hull. They climb. In the carrack's skeleton, they find the steps that lead to a quarterdeck meant for officers, and they descend. Searching the quarters, they find it is mostly bare, with only bed frames, empty chests, and cabinets left behind, relics arranged as if someone might return at any hour. A museum of absence, wood gone brittle with the slow patience of cold. It is a ghost frozen in the glass of its former glory, preserved and forever antiquated. Soon they ascend to the top deck and enter the captain's quarters.

Pushing open the door, inside lay a scene of arrested life. A mattress remains on its frame, a small iron tripod fire pit sits nearby, and a captain's desk is bolted before the stern window like a shrine to past voyages. Artifacts that outlived their possessors.

They return to the officers' quarters, where they set to work with quick, efficient violence. Tearing a bed frame down, levering boards free, smashing chests until planks yielded. The pile of wood for kindling grew; it is a small heap to burn. Inside the captain's quarters again, they use the small iron fire pit, stacking bundles of wood within. Using pieces of fur as tinder, they make a spindle of a shard of wood, spinning it on a board until the friction catches the fur on fire. Hands trembling from cold and exhaustion.

After the fire has burned for some time, they shed their layers. First their fur hood, then head wrap, and lastly their goggles. It is Victoria Frankenstein, 11 years older. Her face beneath looks stranger for its exposure, as if the elements had carved a new person. The air is biting at her skin, but inside the ship a different kind of hunger is fed. Warmth, light, the small sacrament of a flame.

Still mostly bundled up in layers of fur, she opens the messenger bag she carries and pulls out her journal. With a locket chain as a bookmark where she last journaled. She unwraps the leather binding and opens it. Inside is a flat-pressed white lotus flower, withered and shrunken. She turns to the page of the last entry. The date reads:

November 19th, 1805

It's clear she hasn't journaled since that night eleven years ago. She sits in the glow of the iron furnace's fire at the captain's desk. From her satchel, she retrieves a tin cup and a bottle of brandy nearing its end. Pouring a splash of brandy for herself, the fumes linger on the roof of her mouth and in the back of her throat for some time. Then she pulls out a bottle of black ink that appears to be frozen, places it in the tin cup, and sets the cup on the iron furnace to thaw the ink.

Heat finally crept into the room. The frost relents and the ink thaws, pooling black and alive once more. She wraps her furs about her hands as a makeshift gauntlet against the burn and sets the bottle on the desk. With a pour, a cautious bead of brandy meets the ink. "This will keep it from freezing, if only for a short while," she murmurs, more to herself than to the empty room.

She coaxes the quill, stirring the brandy into the ink until the nib drinks its fill. For a long beat, the tip hovers above the paper, poised but reluctant. Victoria's gaze travels distant. Memories play behind her eyes. Salt stings at the rims of her eyelids, and a single tear wavers. Then, with a small, deliberate violence, her eyes slam shut, for she painfully considers what she is about to write. The black ink christens the page of a new entry.

"Winter, 1816. In the event of my demise, these are my last confessions and testaments. I am trapped in the North Pole, drawing nearer to Jan'ry's start. I feel the presence of my doom getting closer. I have discovered this ship frozen in the ice, and I am unable to refrain from making comparisons. This ship was once a magnificent vessel, brilliant and masterfully crafted, filled with dreams and ideals of grandeur to carve a path in history to new discoveries. It was once instrumental in igniting hope among many in the future, only to lie frozen and forgotten by the world. What a cruel yet just fate for something that has potentially stolen the lives of dozens who had pledged their trust within it. We mirror each other in both the adventurous lives we have lived and the icy demise I am soon to share with it. It seems the stars and the planets put repetition in our path to remind us or to make us face the irony of our choices. My choices... I still question my choices. I chose to tamper with life and death; therefore, I created a monster. I know my monster is coming. It's been eleven years since my initial attempt to elude the angry child I gave birth to, but their vengeance was unwavering. Like Pasiphae, forever known as the witch who brought forth a destructive creature, feasting on the lives of mortals. I believed that, deep in the Arctic, I could lure the monster, but it would come at the cost of my own survival. With my rations depleted and my strength fading, I foresee my fate is close at hand, for the cold is the wrath of nature that has no match. This may be my last opportunity to record the terrors of my creation. The lives they took and my regret for what I've done."

Both of her fists pound on the desk. She is as chipped and cracked as unkempt porcelain. Regret-filled sorrow spills out of her wretch while she grinds her teeth in tears. Eyes clenching tightly closed. Victoria is fragile, and she fights to calm herself back into her seat. When her eyes finally relax, she opens them to continue journaling.

"I am devoid of deserving. A storm of gloom has followed me and in time devoured my seasons, where golden autumns lived and gentle, fragile snowfall once made joy soar. Now, I am consumed by the maws of hell, which bleed my life's accomplishments dry and infect the hollow sky, creating a barrier that excludes me from the inherent pleasures of the moon and the sun. I have deprived myself of worth. I replay the carnage and imagine what revenge comes for me. I shed all merit for repentance, and I choose to use my last efforts to document the events that led me to flee across the world to my death. I carry the voices of what once were my friends, my neighbors, and their children. All who'd perished in my monster's wake still haunt me, as they were the spirits I foreordained to destruction. May their existence be known. Geertrudia De Coperslaeger, The woman who housed me and called me sister. Her husband and my dear childhood friend, Jacop De Coperslaeger. Their dear young daughters, Susanna and Madelief De Coperslaeger. Bernardo was the brave man who gave his life to protect his village. A noble man. A man I was coming to love. Forest hugged the hills near the golden inlet of the Zwin North Sea coast. A village once existed in the autumn of 1813, but it has since vanished. Rode Heuvels. I compare my rash, cold, and confined childhood to the freedom enjoyed by the children in this village. Often I felt blanketed with gratefulness to see children safely be children, to never know the cruel shadow cast by witch hunts, a veering ugly world of callous prejudice, and the inability to feel safe from Napoleon's rule that was not so long ago. Those children were so oblivious to the crude black spot in history. It still glows in my memory, for to live in it was to lift you up and spark embers of hope in even the truly desolate and despairing. A quaint little village that prospered despite its lack of resources. Be there, no mistaking, the life of this small village carried wholeheartedly the potential for growth. It could plainly be seen by how nurtured and free the children were. How seldom the children were scolded for simply being children. The fields on hills flourished with the large green leaves of red mammoth fodder beets that rippled for acres with the kiss of every breeze. A farming village where there was a sense of true community. Everyone took part in making their village thrive. Everyone made sure that no one went hungry. Everyone did their part to help one another. In essence, it was perceived by me as an example of a society reaching perfection."

She hunches at the captain's desk, the quill a thin spear in her hand, the little iron tripod at her side guarding its small blaze. The 400-year-old Carrack moaning around her. Timbers groaning with old throats and every draft a furtive thief that leans against the flame, threatening its life. The warmth was a thing of mercies and jeopardies and therefore as precarious as a candle's last breath, and she wrote as though the words themselves might keep a cold death at bay. But for now, Victoria has found a small corner of comfort for someone who arrived with nothing in a hopeless arctic storm.

Chapter 3

Rode Heuvels

The Kingdom of Holland, 1813

Three years earlier.

Victoria stands under a clothesline, her beige sheets catching in the wind like ship sails. Hanging sheets out to dry, she is in a Dutch-made dress that shares the color of dark red earthly clay with a mostly white apron around the skirt that she acquired some time ago as a charitable gift. Picking up another beige sheet out of a wicker basket and hanging it over the line, she stops. Savoring the burning orange light on this windy November day. Occasionally the clouds travel in front of the sun, blocking its warmth, and for a few minutes it pays as a reminder of how much its buttery glow will be missed in the coming months. It is the first time she is experiencing autumn in this village.

Behind her there is a house framed with a brick exterior, a gambrel roof, and centered Dutch doors. The house bears a striking resemblance to the majority of homes found in small villages across the kingdom of Holland. She is captivated by the sight of the red mammoth beet leaves that stretch for acres. She watches the wind run its hands through the clouds, along the fields, and across the trees. She ponders that the time is coming when this place will soon be a world of harvesting in preparation for winter. Just as cold as ocean water, a tidal wave of northern winds stampedes over Victoria. With her eyes closed, she takes in floral and earthy air, and for as long as the wind passes, she is still. Never turning away from the force of nature.

Soon she throws another sheet over the line. Taking a step forward, her foot nudges some rocks. When she looks down, she sees what formations have been made with a few stones and pebbles. Mosaics are formed into the images of a dog and a horse. She is stagnant, peering over the art just before the clatter of small feet skipping can be heard.

"Did I do well?" A child, who appears to be no older than nine, speaks from behind her. "Yes, child." Victoria spiritedly responds, "Very brilliant, child."

She thinks about the stones that have passed through children's hands and reminisces about how shielded her childhood was. She reflects on the comparison of how freely children can play in this village. In this time. How grateful she is to see children safely be children when the world they live in is not made for it.

"Susanna?" Victoria calls out to the girl. Susanna comes to her side, entwining their arms. "Yes, beautiful Victoria?" Victoria, surprised, tilts her head back in laughter. With her hand over her chest, she asks, "Why the compliment, child?"

Susanna shrugs and answers, "I heard my mother telling Father you were a woman of fifty-two. Well, I stomped my foot, and I spoke aloud to my mother and father, protestant. I don't believe they should insult you like that. You are far too beautiful to be a woman in her fifties. But they are not liars. Shortly I believed them. I hope that I am as beautiful as you when I am a woman of fifty."

Victoria, flattered, looks over Susanna's long, broad face. The girl has innocent radiant skin, a wide nose, and blue eyes that gleam bright with all the artistry of stained-glass windows. "Brilliant child, carry with you forever an immortal goodness that ne'er cracks nor parts at the seams, and be nearer to what you carry now, and you will always be beautiful."

From inside the house, the raspy voice of a woman calls out with a Dutch accent in English, "Victoria?! Come, I have a deed!"

Susanna gasps positively excited at the sound of her mother's voice. She unwinds her arm from Victoria's, and with all the agility of a rabbit, dashes inside, calling out to her mother before even entering through the door. Victoria takes one last look at the horizon to see herself reflected back, as the season's changing is her mirror. Like the earth, she is fragile, and her life will soon seek refuge from the cold. But she has found her refuge in the hands of caretakers. The machine of her life built up momentum in her spring and was fueled and greased by her own conducting hands through her summer and autumn to never stop. Her wintering has begun, and she looks on, acknowledging it. Hoping she will allow for it. She needs to put her stubbornness aside and accept that she is getting old. As a cool breeze sends a chill through her, she hopes she can accept it and still have the endurance to enable in action all the knowledge she has obtained. She seeks the strength to fully live through her last season, embracing all of its elusive beauty.

Victoria finally makes her way inside. "Geertrudia, what deed can I be of help with?" Victoria asks. While in a rocking chair, Geertrudia has her daughter Susanna sitting on her knee. Beside the chair stands a smaller girl by the age of seven in a dark brown tweed dress and white bonnet. She is a smaller version of Susanna with plumper cheeks that swallow her eyes up when she grins. As Victoria connects eyes with her, they share a smile together, and Victoria greets her with a "Hello, Madelief."

Madelief walks over to her and reaches her tiny hand out to grip Victoria's dress with stubby fingers, rubbing her thumb across the fabric repeatedly. Geertrudia, who is a slim woman with hands conditioned in toil, has a fixed smile that rests inside her pale complexion under wavy auburn hair that pours out of the sides and back of a sky blue bonnet. Motherly in presence and friendly in manner, she focuses her attention on Victoria as two men enter the front door of the house.

"This evening is nearer to your first arrival one year ago. We wish to celebrate you being with us for one year by cooking you a dinner full of splendor."

Geertrudia's husband is one of the men that entered the house. He is tall and slender with wide shoulders and a plump long nose on an already long oval face. The wrinkles that ripple on the sides of his mouth as he smiles neighbor the crow's feet beside his eyes, hinting that he is close in age to Victoria. He speaks in a British accent from across the house, "No better a reason to have a grand meal."

"Jacop is right." Geertrudia says, "You have grown to be a part of our family. My husband and I cherish you. Our girls look up to you. You are worthy of a feast."

"I am grateful for you." Victoria responds. "There has been no time in my life where I've known so many wholehearted people. Nor have I had better friends than I have had here." In response to Victoria's gratitude, Geertrudia replies, "We are also grateful for you. I have made arrangements to retrieve vegetables from the others in the village. Bernardo has agreed to spare us a few carrots from his garden. Will you do me the chore and go to Bernardo for the carrots he has promised?"

Susanna jumps off her mother's knee to then ask in her soft British accent, "Can I join Miss Victoria on her walk, Mother?" Geertrudia tells her that it is up to Victoria.

Victoria, with a charming smile, gives Susanna a nod and reaches out her palm, gesturing to take her hand. Geertrudia picks up Madelief before saying, "We will get started on dinner while you get carrots from Bernardo."

Just then Jacop can be heard asking the other man he came in with, "Knelis? Where is the axe we keep near the wood?" Knelis has fragile eyes and soft features for a man in his thirties. With both hands he brushes back his long blond hair, and with a thick Dutch accent he responds, "It broke earlier today while I was using it at Gerben's home." Jacop scoffs, "Geertrudia! Your brother broke our axe."

Geertrudia stands up. "It's alright, Jacop; Knelis will go to Ignaas to have us made up two axes in place of the one he broke. Isn't that right, Knelis?"

Knelis nods in agreement as Victoria turns to Geertrudia, "We are off. We shall return soon with carrots."

Victoria and Susanna step out into the street of Rode Heuvels. It looks like a growing village with dirt roads and little brick paving around the foundation of homes and buildings. Their home is near the village entrance, and they pass by where a water well resides. As they head north through the village, Susanna says, "I was lying in the fields a day or two ago. It was me and Madelief. The sun was past noon. We were watching as the clouds swam past, and I thought, what if clouds could talk? I wonder what tales they would have. What they love. What hurts them. What do you think, Victoria?"

"I don't believe the clouds have a love to tell of. Nor do I believe they have pain to share in good company. Clouds are the makings of gentle nature. Peace in the silence is their creation. Peace in silence is all they speak and need." Susanna asks Victoria, "Pray tell, what of you?" Victoria responds, "What of me? Whatever do you mean, child?" Susanna looks up at Victoria with a glow of naivety and asks, "What tales of love do you have to tell? What stories of woe?"

"Plenty!" Victoria says, humored by the whims of this young girl. She has always been secure in her confidence, and such a question would never puncture her ego. She responds with a gentle demeanor, "None of which I wish to ruminate about, for I do not dwell in the realm of my villains. They need no hand in finding me. Mistake it not, for when they do, it will be my realm they are in, and it will be my force of nature they will have to answer to."

Victoria can see out of the corner of her eye that Susanna somewhat pouts and turns her face away to hide it as though she were being disciplined for asking. Victoria stops in the street and kneels down in front of Susanna.

"But just this once I will tell you of a love of mine I had some years ago." They smile at each other like it was their secret. Victoria grabs her hands. "He was gentle, and he appreciated the light of life in people. He would call me the sunlight of his life. You see, he was a sad man as well. It was an illness that plagued his waking life, damning him to the world of night because the sun is what made him sick."

"No." Susanna gasps.

"I'm afraid so. Even being in the shadows of a room that let in a single ray of sunlight blinded his eyes. So I made the quiet midnight hours feel like a world filled with life, just to see him smile."

Victoria stands up, and they continue walking, passing the water well that is in the middle of a beaten circular path at the entrance of the village.

"Where is he now?" Susanna asks. Reluctantly she answers with an obvious lie, "It has been some years since his departure."

"He died?!"

"Yes, you see, he was taken by his illness."

"Oh, Miss Victoria! Both a story of love and woe. What was his name?"

"Voivode. He had lost all the members of his family before he could learn his surname. So all he had was one name."

"Voivode... stupendous." Susanna says it, and it makes Victoria laugh lightly, finding a joy in learning that Susanna knows such a word as "stupendous."

"I wish I had met him. He sounds handsome and charming."

"He was brooding, often quiet, opinionated... He was intelligent and understanding. He made it easy to love him without any worries getting in the way. He was... irresistibly charming... and... at times... terribly sad. He was... beautiful. He was a kind man as well, which in this world is most important to me. I recall he would gift me my favorite flower every year for my birthday."

"What is your favorite flower?"

"A white lotus."

They continue on the condensed streets. Here the houses are closer together, and more of the villagers can be seen working near their homes. There is a pulse where the whole community is actively working for the progress of the village. Victoria can see in almost every person a motivation that contributes to helping the growth of all in the community. She keenly observed that everyone's decisions were made quickly and without doubt. She knew that it wasn't only her small village that moved like bees in a hive. She had seen such activity before in the greater cities of the Dutch Republic during the late 1700s when their trade market was among the richest in the world before Napoleonic rule transpired. Now trades were weak and growth was difficult, but within this village there was a prosperity of hope that drove its life.

Susanna energetically jumps, "You said earlier I do not dwell in the realm of my villains, and I had a thought. I love stories of villains. They are always so much more to me than stories of monsters."

Now caught in confusion Victoria stops in her steps to reply, "Now it is you who must pray tell. I see no separation of the two. How do you perceive such a notion? Art, not both the antagonist?"

"Not to I." Susanna says, "In that story of Little Red Riding Hood, the wolf is clearly a monster to be feared. But all through the story, he wants to convince her that he is not what she thinks. *He is not the monster at all*; he lies. The same is true for all tales of monsters. The Baba Yaga wants children. But, to steal them away to the woods, the monster has to make the children believe it is not a monster. My father tells me the stories he learned in his schooling about the Greek mythos of Heracles. Everyone he faced and defeated had no doubt that the mighty Heracles was their enemy. I possess fascination in villains, as their tales can unfold in various ways. The great lion Heracles faced fought him because it was his nature to kill or be killed. The cyclops was truly only protecting his small corner of the earth where he could live without bother. Most villains know they are the villain; some perceive they are the hero, justifying wrongdoing for the sake of the good. Then there are the ones that cannot see they are doing anything villainous at all. It is quite evident to me that all monsters are the same. Always taking with no end to their evil. Wretchedly repeating their stories where they lie about not being a monster, but they really are. To which no means to ever be human. It's boring!"

"You are quite a brilliant child." Victoria says as they start to walk again. Susanna continues, "I want to learn more about mythos. I have heard the Greek mythos and the Romans. Truly... truly I wish to learn of the Irish and Scottish mythos. What wonders lay waiting there?"

"I know of a few I gladly will tell of." Victoria says to Susanna, to which the child eagerly nods and says, "Yes! Please!"

"Well, Susanna, I can tell you of a goddess that Scottish people would say we are in the presence of. Beira is known as the Queen of Winter and, to some, as the goddess of harvest. They say she made the mountains, carved the creeks, and drinks from a spring of youth to live young and free all year until she ages in winter. 'Tis then when she is as pale as the fields' snow. The winter is her power, what she was made from. She takes from the earth to harvest for herself for the coming year."

They enter off the street through a short gate where a path leads to a small wooden home as Victoria continues, "When she makes her presence known, then it is time to harvest. But she does not come without fear, for there are people who call her by another name."

As Victoria and Susanna reach the door of the small home, it opens before either one can raise a hand to knock. The man who greets them is tall and slim. He is an Italian man with black hair, showing gray on one side. Appearing to be in his 50s, his skin is tight on his long face, where he adorns a bushy peppered mustache. He smiles at them with his half-draped eyelids and immovable eyes and begins to speak in Italian but quickly stops himself to continue to speak in English.

"Victoria... Susanna. Victoria, you warm me like the afternoon sun with your beauty. What do I owe the pleasure to, if not for the act of saying hello?"

"By me, this is the first I hath seen of your heartfelt compliments, Bernardo."

"I trust, dear Victoria, that they are well received."

"In kind, when they will be, I assure you I will voice it."

"I mean no harm of it. Truly."

"Nor do I feel harmed. Your company is still sought by me, dearest Bernardo. Be it understood we are in the presence of Susanna, and she is a child who deserves to be acknowledged. I invite you to compliment me in other ways. In her presence or without. In kind of course."

"Of course. My apologies, Victoria." Victoria is gesturing with her pointer finger down at Susanna, "My apologies... young Susanna."

Susanna nods her head to accept Bernardo's apology, and in the same instance, she turns to Victoria, befuddled. "Why is Mr. Bernardo apologizing to me?"

Victoria and Bernardo share a light laugh, and shortly after, she answers. "Perhaps there is a difficulty in explaining. Rest assured, not knowing the reasoning for the apology is far better than to never receive the one you deserve." Victoria turns her attention back to Bernardo.

"Bernardo, we have come to retrieve the carrots you promised Geertrudia."

"Yes, of course. I thought so of it being the true reason you were here, but I enjoyed playing a fool for a short time, I must admit." Bernardo steps away into his home and then returns with a small burlap sack tied off with a hemp string. As he hands Victoria the sack, he tells her there are five carrots, just as Geertrudia asked for.

It is just then that Bernardo, Victoria, and Susanna notice the romping of feet and noisy ruffling of high-waist skirts. They all turn to see two teenage girls running through the street toward Bernardo's home. They stop at the gate, winded and gasping for air. Bernardo hollers out to them, "Has something happened?"

"Yes, Mr. Bernardo," one of them says in between catching their breath. Victoria walks over to them. "Yvonne? Zoe? What has happened?" Yvonne, a girl of nineteen, and her seventeen year old sister, Zoe, are more than just out of breath. Their eyes red and wet from crying, with tremors still in their voices. They go back and forth, taking turns explaining what the matter is. They speak in English with Dutch accents.

They explain that their mother, Wilhelmina, is the midwife for Ambroos. Her water had broken not an hour ago. After preparing Ambroos to deliver, Wilhelmina began to recognize that something was wrong. Soon Ambroos' cries of pain would be the telltale signs of birthing complications. The two girls look to each other before one of them says, "She didn't know who to go to. You were the only one she could ask. Our father is there trying to convince Pepijn to rear the child into the world... to no avail."

Victoria straightens up and, for a moment, stares above the homes in the sky. "Will you help her?" Yvonne asks as she wipes away at her endless stream of tears.

Victoria looks to them both and takes a few seconds to make eye contact with them one at a time, and without making them wait for a reply any longer, she responds, "Without a doubt."

Victoria, still holding Susanna's hand, exits the gate. She hands Zoe the burlap sack of carrots. "Zoe, take Susanna home and tell Geertrudia to come to her sisters. With urgency. Hurry, go along now." Victoria then turns around to holler at Bernardo, "Mr. Bernardo! I need your assistance in this urgent matter, if you will so oblige."

He nods, agreeing to be of assistance, and Victoria continues, "Good. Please gather your carpentry tools along with any spirits you may have. Meet me at the home of Gerben with haste."

He launches back into his home, closing the door behind him.

"Yvonne," Victoria says as she turns to the young girl again, "I need you to retrieve the root of a yam and the root of a cassava. Do you understand?" She nods yes, and Victoria commands, "Now tell me what I asked you to retrieve."

"Miss Victoria asked me to retrieve the root of a yam and the root of a cassava."

"Brilliant child. Now tell me what I asked you to retrieve again."

"You asked me to retrieve the root of a yam and the root of a cassava."

"Brilliant child! I need you to bring them to me with haste. Bring them straight to Ambroos' home. Now go!" Yvonne goes off running, and Victoria hurries in the opposite direction, heading further into town.

• • • •

INSIDE AMBROOS' HOME, her husband, Gerbin, a young Dutch man, is raising a soaking rag from a bowl of water. The water runs over his fingers as he wrings it out. Taking it over, he gently spreads it across Ambroos' forehead as she lies in a bed that has been placed in the living room. The contractions put her in pain that makes her eyes bulge and her hands shoot to her hips. From the depths of her stomach, she forces out a gut-wrenching scream. Everyone in the room cringes at the sound. At the bedside is Tessa, small-boned and thirtyish. She sits flanked by Wilhelmina the midwife, Anuschka, and two other elder women. The three elders knotted their hands together in prayer at the foot of the bed, warding against what is to come. Behind them stands a woman in her sixties, shoulders set like weathered stone, watching with the quiet gravity of kin.

Across the room, Ignaas looms. Ignass has broad shoulders, an apron charred black from smithing, and a beard with a wheat field's blond. He and Pepijn, a lean farmer in a grime streaked smock, move through a hard, urgent conversation. In low Dutch, Ignaas is trying to convince Pepijn to use the knowledge that he has from assisting the horses in birthing to rear Ambroos' child. Anything that might be lent to Ambroos' hour. However, Pepijn lacks confidence in assisting with the child's birth and quietly protests against Ignaas's suggestion.

While they continue their heated discussion, the front door to the house opens and a middle aged Spanish man named Kasper enters. His hands are still dirt covered from tending to the fields today. He is holding the hand of his wife, Jacintha. She has auburn hair pulled under her white bonnet, and with her head slightly tilted downward, she follows behind her husband. They give a nod to all and stand against the wall at the back of the room.

Ambroos' screams fill the room once again. They could pull tears from the eyes like an audible extraction. Some flinch at her cries of "It hurts! Help me! The pain! Make it stop!"

Her husband, Gerben, caresses her face and holds her hand, trying to soothe her, but he is unsure how much is actually getting through to her. He is on the verge of tears and struggling with his composure.

Anuschka, Wilhelmina's elder mother, takes pause from prayer after one of Ambroos' ground-shaking cries. She announces across the bed in Dutch, "Gerben. Take this time now to say goodbye, for I fear, my child, there may be no time again."

He contemplates that Anuschka might be right. His tears can be held back no more, and he holds Ambroos' hand against his face as he cries like the sun will burn out. He is powerless. Gerben falls weak and crumbles onto the bed's edge. Kasper and Jacintha watch and begin to hold each other closer. Ignaas and Pepijn fumble their shared words mid-conversation at the sound of Gerben falling apart. They watch his back rise and fall with his wailing. Both men become silent and drop their heads.

Wilhelmina tells Ambroos through her weeping, "I'm so sorry. Forgive me, my dear Ambroos." She then falls into Tessa's shoulder, where her wailing is muffled.

The room is filled with tension. Weary anticipation builds like a sickness in everyone, tying their stomachs in knots and making them nauseous for the heartbreak to come. An air thick with change that an era of heavy melancholy descends on them.

Gerben cries to Ambroos, "If ever I have stolen any of your days, I am sorry. If ever I have given you a day without love, I am sorry. Dearest... my dearest Ambroos. Where will love live in this world if you are no longer here? I am sorry ever you wished more of me. You were the reason food was good and the air filled my lungs. Without you... without you, my dearest Ambroos, fire will lose its warmth."

The front door swings open again, and Victoria enters the house. Only Jacintha and Kasper look up while the rest grieve. Wilhelmina feels the light touch of a hand on her shoulder. She looks back to see Victoria standing over her. "Oh, Victoria, I did what I could."

Victoria reaches over to feel Ambroos' stomach. In shifting her hand, she says, "Worry not. There is still time." Victoria raises her voice to get the attention of the room. "There is still hope. Gerben! With your approval, I would like to conduct an operation that has seen the survival of both the mother and child. An operation that has been practiced in the African region of Uganda for hundreds of years. I know this operation to be reliable. With help... I can save the life of your wife and child."

"Then there is no time to waste!" Geertrudia says from the open door. Standing with her are Jacop and Zoe. Victoria looks to Geertrudia, acknowledging her, and then to Gerben, who gives her a nod of approval.

"Ambroos," Victoria says lightly as she grabs her hand, "You are the only person in this room for whom their wants truly matter. I trust myself. I know myself to shatter disbelief upon reaching the fruition of my ambitions. Grant me your trust and tell me this is what you want, and I will hesitate no longer."

Ambroos, heaving in pain, fights to look at Victoria. Ambroos is assessing; sweat is stinging her eyes, and pain is drilling through her chest and up her neck. "Miss Victoria... I grant you my trust. Do what you must... but against all odds... save my baby. If nothing else... th-that... is all I truly want."

Victoria then faces everyone in the room. The room tightens like a held breath. Victoria turns, the low light throwing her face into a mask of calm that holds a blade's edge. "There are no certainties in this," she says. "I will take full responsibility for Ambroos and her child. I need only a few to help."

Bernardo crosses the threshold with his carpentry kit. Victoria's eyes flick to him and then to Geertrudia. "Tessa, Geertrudia. Four buckets from the well. Quickly." She points at Bernardo. "You and

Ignaas, burn the tools in the smith's fire. Anything with the field on it must leave. Those who stay must be washed and promise not to interfere." Her voice is plain, iron-forged. She speaks with the vigor of a captain on her hundredth voyage. "Trust me, and there is hope."

Outside, the well complains as Tessa and Geertrudia haul bucket after bucket, their shoulders straining, the rhythm of the crank's waning parts repeating like a song.

Inside, the air tastes of wood and damp linens. Jacintha, Zoe, and Wilhelmina sit frozen, faces drained of color, watching Victoria set her instruments with the deliberation of a professional barber or surgeon.

Bernardo returns with his tools singed in his hands. "Anything else?" he asks. Yvonne slips in, palms dark with roots. "Miss Victoria. I have them."

"Clean them. Crush it with only water. Nothing else. Do not stop until you hath made a paste of it." Victoria's orders fall like lightning, crisp and immovable, efficient and without doubt. Jacintha, Zoe, and Wilhelmina spring into motion, pounding the roots until the kitchen smells faintly of earth and something bitter. Victoria gives Ambroos wine without ceremony. "Drink when you need," she murmurs. Ambroos drinks until her eyelids soften and the wine unknots some of her terror.

The women return with the buckets. Victoria washes the blades and her hands, then guides Wilhelmina and Bernardo through the same ritual. As a hygienic practice, Victoria makes it mandatory if they are to assist her in the procedure.

She wipes Ambroos' belly with cool water, observing her all the while for signs of further intoxication. Victoria's pause narrows and then snaps as Ambroos sinks into a stupor. Victoria's voice, now a small, clear bell, announces, "It is time."

Bernardo on one side, Wilhelmina on the other, Victoria brings the blade down and cuts Ambroos' lower abdomen. She moves through the body with navigation and finesse, making incisions through multiple layers one after another. First skin, then fat. When she reaches the muscle, she cuts it vertically, pushes it aside, and uses hooks to have Wilhelmina and Bernardo pull the muscle open slightly. Another layer of tissue is exposed. Another cut, and another set of hooks then occupies both of their hands.

Victoria is at a point where she must operate with no further assistance. She reaches in through the muscle and tissue to the uterus wall. Another cut. With her hand, she separates the incision so she can see the amniotic sac. One more layer. She is slow, cutting only the layer of tissue and nothing more. Just one more layer deeper... into Ambroos' body... with a carpenter's blade.

Ambroos feels her intestines on the outside of her body. She is awake, flushed with vulnerability, and pouring tears. With her eyes closed, she feels Gerben holding her tight-gripped hand. Skin, fat, and muscle parted. Each layer surrenders with a wet, uncompromising, gritty truth. Bernardo and Wilhelmina hold hooks that bite into Ambroos' flesh, hands obeying Victoria's commands. In reaching the uterus, she works with a terrible tenderness, vividly measured, impossibly patient. The kind of patience that keeps a flame alive in a storm.

Ambroos lies in a half-conscious state, her awareness narrowed to the peculiar sensation of feeling Victoria's breaths inside her stomach. Gerben's hand squeezes hers, a small anchor in the dark. "Gerben," she says in a breath, like a ghost moaning his name, and he bends nearer, shoulders bracing for whatever comes. She is suspended in a drunken purgatory, aware of every slice of her flesh and the powerless discomfort of feeling her insides held by hands for the first time. All she can do is look up at him through drowning, half-lidded eyes.

Then, slowly, Victoria begins to pull the infant's head through the incision. A grueling, guttural moan rises from Ambroos, scraping the air, pain made elemental. A small, slick head emerges. A child is in

Victoria's hands.

Wilhelmina takes the newborn. Victoria snips and ties the cord with knitting string. "Gerben." Her voice conveys a sense of blessing and transfer. "Your daughter."

Ambroos' breath hiccups. "Why... she isn't crying," she whispers.

Victoria answers softly, like a gentle morning wake up, "A moment. You will hear her soon."

Then the world changes. A single, fierce cry bursts from the infant. A bright, tearing sound that floods the room like sunlight through rain. Relief comes so suddenly it feels physical. Shoulders slump, and tears release in noise. Ambroos' face breaks open at the sound. "That is the most beautiful sound I've ever heard," she says, astonished.

Gerben lowers their child toward her, voice thick. "It is beautiful because you already love her."

Victoria listens to the new parents as she cleans her hands for the next part of the procedure. She remembers loving someone so much that everything they did seemed beautiful. She thinks of when she was expecting a child and the days she counted down to when she would hear their cries. The memory's joy becomes fleeting, and she resents herself.

Victoria expeditiously begins work on closing Ambroos. She instructs everyone to patiently wait outside while they start sewing her open wounds shut.

When the last knot is tied, she massages the yam and cassava paste into the seam, the simple alchemy of root and water sealing what has been split. Jacop's uncertain voice drifts through the doorway, asking if Ambroos will live.

Outside the house, waiting, are Wilhelmina's two young daughters, Zoe and Yvonne, and her husband, Ignaas. Huddled next to them are the four elder mothers and Geertrudia alongside Tessa. Kasper and his wife, Jacintha, stand stress-ridden with the group, holding each other.

"I hope to see them both survive," Ignaas says. "Poor is the man,

Gerben. He will have no choice but to know pain, losing one or the other. Rode Heuvel has not seen the loss of a child in three years. Not since you, Kasper and Jacintha, when you lost your seven-year-old daughter."

"Isabelle," Geertrudia says.

"Yes, Isabelle, may God rest her soul." Ignaas nods in sadness.

"This terror is in the same vein, as it holds such a close remnant to Isabelle and how we still mourn losing her," Geertrudia recalls to Jacintha, who is touched and reaches to hold her hand. Jacintha says lowly, in an unused voice, "Happen what may, we will remain strong, as we will have each other in any darkness."

Victoria steps outside into a congregation of held breaths. The young cluster, hands knotted together. Elder mothers stand like weathered pillars. She looks into the circle of faces, into the raw, bright hope that has gathered there.

"Ambroos will heal," Victoria says. "She will live, and she will watch her daughter grow."

Joy and relief erupt as if someone had thrown open a dam. Zoe and Yvonne cry out and then laugh; the elder mothers sob and laugh all at once. Geertrudia charges forward, emotion tearing her features free, and wraps Victoria in an embrace that feels more like "celebrate with me" than "thank you." Jacop rests a hand on Victoria's shoulder. The girls Yvonne and Zoe cling to her as well. From the back, Ignaas' voice rises, plain yet heartfelt, "You are an angel of life, Victoria."

For a small pocket of time, the whole village holds that sound. The sound of a falling tide of fear replaced by a flush of triumph and a sweetness that makes the chest ache. In the room where terror lived minutes before, a newborn breathes, a mother opens her eyes to love, and the people who have watched history take from them again and again reach for one another and find themselves bright with relief. The moment tastes like victory, life endures, and joy pours through the seams.

"You are an angel of life, Victoria." As she hears Ignaas say that, her eyes shoot shut. Her indifferent demeanor crumbles away. Droplets drip out between her lashes, and a euphoric stinging happens under her eyes.

Jacop wraps his arms around Geertrudia and Victoria. In this moment, she observes the heart of the little village growing stronger. That new life has joined their communal family without losing Ambroos in the process. There is but a short moment where she absorbs how moved these people have become, the impact she has made on their lives because they needn't suffer loss on this day. A short moment passes before the flash of a lightning strike replays in her mind, revealing the blackness of the silhouette in her memories. Here she returns to her nightmares of the monster she created, climbing out of the fire and absorbing the light into the abyssal darkness it carries. She thinks to herself as she watches these people celebrate in this moment, "I am burdened with frustration at how I devalue what little good I do in this world, for I am undeserving of the praise for the atrocity I committed. In the late hours I sorrow in thought of what poor souls suffer now to the hell I unearthed upon this land."

Chapter 4

A Woman In The South Of France

A red leather bound journal tied closed rests on Victoria's lap. She sits in her bare room, which contains only her bed and a trunk of clothes. Sitting on her bed, she stares at the wall where the afternoon sunlight lies. The light breeze entering through her open window lifts the curtains. The air carries a strong scent of the field found just outside the village. The scent chills her nose, and it reminds her of a woman she used to know. It was during a time she spent in the South of France when she was twenty-four. Perhaps this is a good time of day to take a walk and ruminate for a while if she is going to think on young love.

Victoria heads downstairs, and before reaching the bottom step, Susanna and Madelief can be heard laughing with each other and parading through the house in their clogs, Dutch-styled wooden shoes. They were clacking against the wood boarded floors with their running. Upon entering the room, she looked at the clogs. Susanna's are red, and Madelief's are a fair blue. Geertrudia comes inside from the back door; her arms are soaked and covered in suds.

Victoria calls out to her, "Geertrudia? Let me carry some of your load. Is there enough work from Ambroos' and Gerben's clothes that I may help you with the wash?" Geertrudia casually dries her arms off, rubbing them down against her apron that she has tied around her waist. As she does, she gives Victoria an earnest smile where her cheeks swallow up her eyes.

Victoria recognizes that little Madelief shares the same qualities in her smile. Geertrudia maintains a high spirited presence even during strenuous labor. With a worked up sweat, she replies, "No. Don't you worry about any of that, Miss Victoria. I'm still so grateful for you taking care of Ambroos."

Susanna and Madelief run up to Victoria on either side, Susanna wrapping around her arm and Madelief grabbing hold of her skirt. The girls laugh and giggle about it. Victoria gives the girls a smile and then turns her attention back to Geertrudia, "I am just as grateful I was of help. But please allow me to assist you somehow."

With endearment, Geertrudia remarks, "You are such a sister to me. How I adore you, Victoria. How about a walk with the girls? They could use the play, and I would be the happier to be without the hammering of clogs for a short while."

Geertrudia starts a laugh that Victoria joins her in. Susanna jitters excitedly with the idea, and Victoria responds, "We will take a walk through the fields then... maybe twice, for your mother's sake." This ignites the young girls into a jumping fit that explodes with the clatter of wooden clogs.

• • • •

THERE IS A PATH WOVEN in the dirt around the fields. The red mammoth beets comfortably sit under the leaves' shade. Susanna and Madelief freely frolic close to Victoria. She stares at the fields and the yellowing of the red mammoth beet leaves. Every time the wind picks up, Victoria times her breath so she may breathe in deep to catch what new scent rides the draft. The air is as cooling as river water, while the sun is a gentle, hugging warmth.

The fields remind her of her time in Gevaudan, France. The wet dew that would linger on the morning world. How it would drip from every flower petal and blade of grass. She thinks about how in the evenings the bugs would join together to serenade the setting sun. She can't remember a moment during her time there when she didn't enjoy the weather. Even when it would rain, it was always welcoming and comfortable. She describes the rising petrichor as having a powerful fragrance, which she refers to as "the smell of rain."

Then she remembers Simone's face; the way Simone fully surrendered herself was evident in the way she kissed. The first kiss they shared took place in the rain. Victoria smiles with a blush as she reminisces about the woman from Gevaudan. Simone Plourde.

Her name painted pictures of a clear and starry night sky in Victoria's memories. A woman raised from childhood to know only a life in the country. Her wild dark brown hair was always tied up in a bun. Her cynical remarks knew no mercy for any such person, place, or object. All of life was pain, and she reminded everyone to never forget it. But Victoria knew there was an untouched heart within her that was eager to be felt. Simone longed to finally see the energy she used for anger be used instead to love. How fiercely she would love if she were ever sought after. Before they ever touched lips, she was not sure Simone could tell that her heart beat with all an army's percussion each time they grew nearer. Nor could Victoria read Simone. There were initial moments of undeniable goodness that sparked a desire to pursue her heart, but Simone's heart was a brooding one, with much downtrodden dismay to express. If there was ever a moment where she displayed affection for Victoria early in their friendship, it was hidden well behind a rough facade. Victoria will never know what inspired Simone that night and why she grabbed her face to kiss her. There was a passion there that had built up so much she could feel that it was unbearable for her to refrain from any longer.

She can remember Simone's eyes when she pulled back to look at her, boggling and barely visible in the dark, fraught with fear that her actions were wrong. Simone did not realize how fearless Victoria truly was. A Frankenstein who always took what they wanted in life. A young Victoria in her twenties stares back at Simone with a rising passion and excitement, contemplating pulling Simone back to her. She tells herself in her head, "Death follows Frankensteins," and then pulls Simone in for an embrace. Drenched, they tightly hold each other close. Simone began to cry with alleviation that she was well received.

Victoria thinks to herself, "I had found, with impossible luck, another soul whose kindness merited kindling. This kindness was much like that of my first young love. Except for that time I discovered it within another woman. She was a woman who risked her life with the act of a kiss. A woman who secretly stood in her inflections outside the paths set forth for women. I had found another... other. It has been twenty years, and in that time much reflection has transpired. I was in love with Simone. She was like the stars to me. Often hiding in the dark and overlooked in the presence of the moon, but given attention, they could be loved for their wonder. Regrettably, like the stars, she travels with a condemnation to one day rapidly burn out. One less light to observe in wonder as all of night forever grows darker."

Susanna screams! Victoria abruptly returns to the present, realizing she had momentarily forgotten that she was walking with the girls. Susanna's giggling soon follows as the girls continue their ongoing tickle match. Victoria watches their white cotton Dutch caps bob up and down as they trot, skip, and run in circles. Today their dresses are identical, like most days, with Madelief's being about two sizes smaller.

Victoria enjoys their presence, and it does not hinder her ruminations. Her understanding and patience are bottomless; they go beyond merely tolerating children to include a deep appreciation for witnessing a child experience the essence of living. It is bottomless how much she adores children. She has always been lucky to be paying attention the way she does and has seen many times children experience the short moments that make childhood memorable. Children can travel with wonder, flying wildly from one blind plan of joy to the next. No, they are of no bother, and Victoria laughs off the scare.

Continuing in her thoughts, she ponders about how crops and farmland always remind her of Simone. This is the second time in the past few days that she has found herself revisiting the memories of a past love. Maybe it has something to do with Bernardo. He has voiced quite an interest in the past few weeks. Maybe it is his presence that uncovers these thoughts. It is admirable that even though Victoria is the reason that his pursuit has been playfully drawn out and time consuming, he persists, and this makes her think that he can maintain an interest, which is flattering to her. She knows that Italians and the English have plenty of differences in their customs, and maybe he is afraid to stumble on one that causes disrespect. Alternatively, he may simply be too gentle to make any advances in his pursuit of her. Nonetheless, she believes they should spend some time getting to know each other if this slow bloom is to feel healthy in its ascension. She stops. She stops walking. She stops thinking. Her next thought to arise is, "Is it time? Can it be time... to let love flourish once again?" she asks herself, knowing she is still far from feeling as powerful a spirit as love, for Bernardo. But these ideas of courting a partner, they lead to time spent in the presence of another giving up themselves. In those waking hours when a person makes themselves vulnerable for another, that is where love tends to grow.

Victoria and the girls soon return to the village. It is a bright day out, with the aroma of frost in the northern winds making the approaching winter apparent. As they reach the entrance, they can see that the village is active as many are getting their daily tasks done. Pepijn is taking a break from keeping up the stables to retrieve water from the well.

Knelis, standing in front of the blacksmith's workshop, is swiping his straight hair out of his eyes. He then picks up two freshly made axes that he takes across the village entrance.

Pepijn pulls the bucket from the well and uses his hand to cup the water to drink it. In doing so he loses his balance, but Knelis is there to pull him back, avoiding a fall into the well. Pepijn starts laughing as he shows Knelis his gratitude with a few hearty pats on the back.

Benji, the local fisherman, leaves a wrapped bundle of fish at a nearby house. Most likely he has recently returned from a fishing trip and is delivering a requested catch. Even from this distance Victoria can tell it is Benji the fisherman, not because of his height or his reddening leather skin but because he carries around a load of feeble, wretched years. No one person can say he is unpleasant to deal with since he already makes himself scarce; therefore, it's difficult to speak ill of a man who is never seen. Still, Victoria finds much to analyze about someone who presents themselves as unwelcoming. She and the girls meet with Knelis before the house. Always such a quiet man, he smiles and nods to greet them all.

"Knelis? Where may I find Jacop at this hour?" Victoria asks. He raises his arm and points across the way. "The blacksmith shop?" she questions. He smiles and nods in response. "Thank you, Knelis. Girls. Follow your uncle home."

She walks over to the blacksmith's shop and steps inside to see Jacop and Ignaas talking. Ignaas reaches up to dip his hands in a bucket of water that he hangs on a hook from the ceiling.

Jacop greets her with a, "Good day, Victoria. How are you this afternoon?"

"Reminiscent, in fact. I had a thought. "If you don't mind, I would like to pull you away from Ignaas for a moment."

"Not at all. Ignaas. I will return shortly." The two of them leave Ignaas in his shop to step outside together. "What can I assist you with, Victoria?" Jacop asks with serious inquiry.

"Back in England, when you were my family's financier, I requested that you take on a task to travel to France. Do you recall?"

"I recall, yes."

"In your travels did you ever meet with Simone Plourde?" Jacop thinks on it for a moment before answering. "I do not recall her presence. It was the oldest. A young lad and four other children, I believe. No Simone that I recall. What raises the question?"

Victoria replies with a smile, "I felt I could not think on anything but the past as of today. My old friend came up in my memories, and

I couldn't keep from my curiosities of how your dealings with her transpired."

"Well, I'm sure when she returned home she was pleased to see you took care of her family." Jacop reassures Victoria, who nods agreeably. Jacop takes a moment to study her. Seeing the mild disappointment that claims her features worries him.

"Is there anything more you wish to discuss?" he asks expectantly. Victoria's eyes shoot up to meet him. "No, nothing more. I just never found the time to ask of her until now."

With a concern in his voice, he says, "I've never known you to hide your intentions away. Professionally speaking, verily, I know it is not my place to pry, but as your oldest friend, I see you have tucked so much of yourself away in the crevices of your thoughts. You have been with my family and me for some time now, and I am all the happier to have you with us. But I gather the sense that you have changed, much further beyond the normal pains of life and experience." Every word spoken with earnest intention.

Victoria can recall the day they met in Bruges a year ago. How serendipitous to have crossed paths. She had been traveling for years, living off the kindness of strangers. Trying to balance between survival and societal politeness so as not to overstay a welcome. It seemed that her body moved mechanically during this time due to exhaustion so deep that it had buried itself in her bones. She gave little answer and half truths when Jacop asked what came of her and the fate of her home. She should have known better than to think it was a substantial answer for him.

Ever since she and Jacop became reacquainted, he has explained that his father and mother passed away nearly a decade ago. He told her of his sister, who met an unfortunate demise in an untimely accident. He had not seen any of his family since he left his life in England. He was the Frankenstein family's financier, a position he resigned from to move to the Dutch Republic in 1802 to marry Geertrudia.

Long past memories still live with the vitality of when Victoria's father would bring her to Jacop's family home. Weekly trips to discuss business with Jacop's father.

In their childhood friendship they shared notes on subjects, for they both studied under the same private tutor for lessons such as piano and history. They spent significant time in his family's library, which was an important part of their childhood and where they often enjoyed each other's innocent banter. "I can still remember the way his soft, boyish face looked," Victoria contemplates, revolving between his appearance from then and now. "Even with laborious wrinkles of his older years finely pressed into his features. While he stands in front of me, his hand is lightly resting over his stomach, serving as a brace to remind him of his proper composure. An order he keeps refined so that he never forgets his lessons in mannerisms. Just like when he was a boy." The thought pulls a one sided grin out of her. "I can see the deepened cracks in his fingertips where the skin has dried, a testament to his long hours spent working in the fields, with the villagers, and in his home. And though his hands may be strong, they are no longer boyish, evident our friendship is an old one and more so that there is little that has survived from when we were young but that of whence our friendship came. We are each other's oldest remaining fellowship. Quite the rarest of friendships to uphold."

Victoria assures Jacop, placing her hand on his arm, "What you have observed rings some truth, Jacop, and I wholeheartedly apologize for any concern it may have caused. There is a lifetime of woes that are best kept in the shadows of time, lest it take away from the second chance that has been bestowed upon me here and now. I have much to enjoy, all thanks to you and yours." Urging him to believe all is well. Jacop gives a reluctant nod, not all too convinced that there is nothing more than the curious inquiry, but accepting that all is as well as she claims. "I will see you at home," she says, bidding farewell.

Continuing her walk, Victoria passes through the streets, and just as she is about to come upon Bernardo's house, he steps out his front door. He has in one hand a wooden tool carrying case. It only takes him a short single glance to detect her strolling by. As he closes the door behind him, he yells to her, "Victoria!" She stops to wave, and in seeing him come towards her with purpose, she waits still for him to arrive.

"Victoria. The whole of my day will be fraught with duties. I am quite glad to have been gifted with even a chance to see you." He reaches for her hand to hold it for a moment. It is far less than a handshake and not nearly firm enough to feel like she was being forced to simply hold his hand. Delicately, Bernardo holds her hand up between them with her fingers latched over his. He continues, "Even for a glance, it shall be enough of a meal to fill my heart. I pray I may not be starved of you; come tomorrow."

Victoria's brows lift together until there is nowhere left for them to go. As she bashfully closes her eyes, she asks, "Pray tell, what duties keep you today?"

Bernardo lets go of her hand. Their fingers, having only touched for a few short seconds, now come apart. In that short time, Victoria could feel her heart beat a hundred thousand times. She could feel a cooking warmth rise in her chest and a hot flash fill her face. She struggled against her desire to be closer to his body. The amount of restraint she found in order for her self-discipline to prevail was at first in need of scrounging. She felt strange having so many things occur in that small moment where she touched his fingers. Perhaps, she notices, it's because she had stopped breathing. As she inhales a breath, she thinks to herself, "I have put soup to boil and hath been done with it sooner than the length of holding his hand felt."

Bernardo replies to her, "I must rebuild the steps in the home of Kasper and Jacintha. Their two sons have seemingly worn them down to be unbearable. I must be on my way. I will see you again soon."

Briefly she watches him walk down the street and then continues on. Her walk has led up to Ambroos and Gerben's home. She sees Gerben step outside.

"Good afternoon, Victoria." Gerben says "pleased" and waves.

"Good afternoon, Gerben. I have come by to see that Ambroos is healing properly."

"Ah yes. You are welcome to go inside and see, but I cannot stay. It is expected of me by Albertus to be at the windmill. He has asked for mine and Jacob's help today." Victoria nods in understanding as he passes by, and she walks inside to see Ambroos asleep with her newborn daughter on their bed, which is still placed in the living room. Victoria walks up to her bedside quietly. She sees they are both resting comfortably. Watching over them in reverence for the gentle nature of Ambroos nurturing her baby, she decides not to disturb them. Lingering enough to bring a longing tear to her eye, she turns to leave. She wipes away the tears just as fast as they fall. There it is in her vision of life, what she defines as a world half grey. To feel only half joy, feel only half warmth, and smell faint all the perfumes of the world because she lives a life of wanting what she knows she can never have.

"Victoria," Ambroos utters in a hoarse voice. Victoria turns back and whispers, "Ambroos. I come to see how you were healing. I will return the day after tomorrow.

Ambroos replies, "I'm healing. My darling husband makes sure of my rest. He is a good man." Victoria smiles at her. "Verily, that is good. Good. What have you named her?"

"We have not decided on one yet. Umm... Misses?"

"Yes, Ambroos?"

"I ponder of you often. How I wish to thank you for that which you have done. How does a woman come to know that which you know?"

"I learned it, my friend. A long time ago. Taught to me by "Other" women."

"You must tell me on some day what else you have learned. Teach me what I should know. For I hope that some day, my daughter shall be as wondrous as you. Pray tell, how does a woman become a doctor as you have?"

Victoria gives pause before answering as she realizes the truth in what she plans to say.

"I am not a doctor. Where I came from, women... are not allowed to study in universities. Therefore, I can never obtain as high a title, such as doctor." Victoria nods while smirking with self-disappointment.

"Get your rest now." Victoria says.

"Victoria," Ambroos raises her head to look into Victoria's eyes with her tired ones.

"You are a wondrous woman." Victoria nods, accepting her compliment, be it reluctantly, and tells Ambroos, "Yes, as are you. Rest now, dear. We shall visit again in good time."

Without needing further convincing, Ambroos nestles close to her baby. Victoria allows herself only a second to admire the sight of mother and child. A sight she has seen over the years in medical studies and travels, yet now in this moment is less nostalgic and more foreign to observe. The tender love of a new life was nothing short of incredible.

Chapter 5

A Future Made By Kind Children

It is so early the sun has not risen, and a cold dawn fosters frost on the grass and the vapors of Victoria's breath. She walks in the north just outside of the village on a dirt trail. It is a path that leads to a small schoolhouse with bones that look to be pushing 200 years. A tall structure with a single room, large enough to hold a town gathering. Victoria steps inside when Susanna and Madelief push past her, stopping to hand her yellow chrysanthemum flowers. One flower each, Susanna and Madelief hand them to her one at a time. The chrysanthemums are an art of nature with bold yellow hues and radiant, vivid textures, with both flowers sharing a deep blossom. They clearly picked them with keen thought and care.

With an elegance and fragility that she reserves for children, Victoria gracefully accepts the flowers, and Susanna and Madelief sit at their desks.

As Victoria walks to the front of class, there is no other sound that can be heard in the room except for the floorboards grimly moaning under her steps. She possesses a stern authority rooted in unwritten laws and unspoken vows, which, although she never articulates to maintain control, earns her unquestionable respect from most, particularly the children.

After putting the flowers in a vase, with several other flowers that the girls had gifted her many days prior, she turns to the class with an enthusiastic demeanor.

The youngest is Madelief, seven, her face still a map of unpracticed wonder; Susanna follows at nine. Three girls cluster between ten and twelve, their laughter feathery soft. The two sisters, Yvonne and Zoe, sit close together, almost inseparable at times. It is with five boys, all in their teens and pressed near the others in age, that complete the restless constellation of students. As Victoria starts to speak, she is just as quickly interrupted by Yvonne, "Miss Victoria?"

She gives glances to other students who are wide eyed, which Victoria reads into, concerned.

"We... want to know... if... you could teach us..." Just then Kasper walks in with his son, Augusto, a young man of sixteen. They both stand by the door, hesitant to step further, as if they were intruding. Kasper grips his straw hat in front of his farming smock with soil covered hands. His body bent in embarrassment. Vulnerability pours from his body language, in fear of being turned away.

In a Spanish accent, Kasper interrupts the conversation, "Fair Mistress Victoria. Is there room for my son in your lessons? I hope to pull him out of the fields so that he can attend your lessons in the mornings from now on.

"It too is my wish to be here, Mistress Victoria." Augusto innocently adds. Victoria responds in Spanish, "Of course. There is plenty of room."

"Ah, you speak Spanish as well!" Kasper remarks with newfound confidence. "I thank you, Mistress Victoria. Augusto, take your seat, my son. Learn you shall." He gently pats Augusto's cheek affectionately.

After Kasper leaves, Augusto has settled into a nearby desk. Victoria says to Yvonne, "As I was saying, there is only one lesson a day. Let us not be too hasty, and today we shall continue with grammar." But before Victoria can continue, Yvonne speaks up again, "All of us are interested in learning about..." Victoria looks over all the children in the classroom before Yvonne continues, "Well, we are keen to learn about trust."

"Trust?" Victoria questions with both her eyebrows arching high, "I think we can humor this for a little while. The definition of trust is not something that will take up an entire lesson."

"No," Yvonne says, "not the definition but instead the knowledge of how to bestow trust upon a man. My father deals in trade every couple of months. Men who travel from other ports come through to trade with him. I heard them talk about how everyone in the Dutch Republic is suspicious of each other. We live in a world of fear. I have heard the tradesmen speak of it. They speak of sisters who have come to denounce their brothers, sons who have denounced their fathers, and friends who suspect each other of being traitors. A traitor to the traditions of the Dutch people. The Dutch Republic. A traitor for not resisting the tyrant, Napoleon, and his rule. Rode Heuvels has not seen the Agents De Police or even one French Imperial soldier in over a year. That is not to say the rest of our Dutch people are not still suffering. The elites find no exclusion for their sons, who were taken from them to join the imperial army. No one trusts anyone. How do we trust?"

Victoria walks away from her desk to be closer to the students. Looking over the eyes of the children, it's as if they all asked and now sit in wait for their answer.

"I see," she responds to Yvonne, to then spend a moment in silence with the classroom. As she leans against her desk, she addresses them, "There is no short answer in such a request. I can give many answers, and I can give my answer. The one answer that holds meaning with me. Even so, few in this class will grasp my words. This subject is equally a profoundly important matter and a difficult one to navigate." Augusto gently interjects, saying, "Mistress Victoria, if I may, instruct us nonetheless. The eldest of us can do our part to learn it. Therefore, we can do our part to teach it to the youth among us."

His classmates unanimously agree with him. Victoria is speechless at her student's eagerness. She ponders intensely, piecing together a strategy with her collective knowledge like a chess player planning their next four moves. She straightens up and speaks with the well versed melody of a string quartet.

"Humankind survived thus far due to fear. Before society, before the warmth of clothes, and before the safety of shelter, mankind dreaded the beasts that were greater and mightier than themselves. It is fear for which we eventually built shelters. We feared hunger, illness, and death in the winter. It is fear that to which we began farming and harvesting for the winter months. We feared losing water to which we then settled our homes close to the rivers and oceans. It is because of fear we can recognize what to trust. It is why we tell stories of woe. Of monsters and villains. So that our next in lineage may heed the telltale signs of what to fear. In turn crystallizing more and more of what to trust. Folklore and books provide examples of poor decisions and villainy. It is more than just bedtime stories and amusement. It is a form that must be acknowledged to facilitate the transfer of ethical and moral lessons about humanity and the understanding of villainy. These lessons can be found further in the study of historical documents as well. The history of kings and queens provides valuable insights into this form. The better you recognize poor decisions and villainous traits, the better you use your fear to avoid or evade them. Fictitious characters such as the big bad wolf from Little Red Riding Hood describe untrustworthy traits to look for in what can be a villainous person. The dangers posed by a stranger's deceptive politeness are significant. Who here knows The Song of Lord Halewijn, or *Heer Halewijn?*"

All but Augusto raise their hands, and Victoria continues, "A maiden hears a song in the night. The lure of Lord Halewijn, and she becomes enchanted. She knows that all young maidens who have sought this enchanting lord were never to return. Still, she is swooned and wishes to seek him out. With only the permission of her brother, who makes her promise that so long as she keeps her integrity intact by taking a sword so she may protect herself in case misfortune should befall her, then she has his blessing. She then pursues the lure of Lord Halewijn deep in the woods. When she finds him, she cries, satisfied with the man he is and the loving, gentle nature he portrays. Soon they ride further into the labyrinth of the woods, where he leads her to a gallows field." Victoria recites a verse:

Then they arrived at the gallows field,
with many women's corpses hanging there.
with many women's corpses hanging there.'

Victoria continues speaking as normal, "This is the importance of the story. In this moment we must recognize that no maiden has ever returned to her home and family because the Lord Halewijn lured them all to their murder. It is here in the story that our fair maiden flourishes in her strength to stay true to her integrity and moves forward with vigor to act swiftly against her villain. She acts as such because she portrays the idol of what must be done by us, the listeners of her story, or in good time, we will fall victim to deception. Our maiden challenges him to death by combat, and while he is distracted by her ruse, she beheads Lord Halewijn with the sword she bared. Our maiden was the only one to return home. Many a maiden had to fall in order for fear to rise within our maiden. 'Twas fear that led her to her survival. The Song of Lord Halewijn is a lesson we sing about to remind all that the paths of curiosity can be traveled until our survival is threatened. We sing to remind us to fear not death until we foolishly tempt it. We sing to remind the children who are yet to come that there is no trust where there is harm and to see with all your integrity when your trust is in danger of deception. Fear the knight or the lord, as in our fair maiden's story; fear them who enchant us with whims and loving satisfaction but with the same hands will harm others. It is with those words that I wish you to grow, remembering to feed a world where truth is greater than all those who choose to deceive. If you are to be, then you will build a world in which there is less deception. There will always be fear; thus, truly unnerving is a world where we must fear without rest from it. Even worse, if what we are to fear is so masked by deception that we no longer know how to recognize what should be feared, then not only will men, women, and children fall, but so shall kings, for you cannot rule a world that can no longer survive."

Yvonne raises her hand and Victoria calls on her to speak.

"Miss Victoria, I was present yesterday when Ambroos was in labour. Why... why did my elders and parents place trust in you? Mine mother sent me to find you, yet I knew not the cause. Soon, I realized that you possessed knowledge that others have yet to gain. Is knowledge worthy of trust?"

Victoria smiles at Yvonne, but before Yvonne can respond, Zoe interjects with an answer: "It's because she is the angel of life." I heard Father call you that."

Victoria is moved almost to tears. She collects herself and replies to Yvonne, "Yvonne, I was trusted because the knowledge I convey is done with vigor. I worked with confidence which assisted in every one in the room trusting me. Understand, because I sought out Ambroos' wishes, because I was considerate with good intent, everyone found within themselves more reason to trust me. This is most important of all... I would never have gone through with the operation had there been a void of trust held in me by Ambroos. We shall not forget; I, in turn, put my trust in everyone there. We needed each other to save Ambroos and her babe."

SOMETIME LATER VICTORIA lets out the day's school session, and while watching the children walk back to the village together, their laughter echoes. Bernardo surprises Victoria by saying, "I'm afraid sometimes." She jumps only slightly and quickly recovers to respond to Bernardo with a little chuckle, "You! You, Mr. Bernardo. What could you be afraid of?"

He replies, "I'm afraid these children don't know pain. Without it they wont seek fantastic elements. What imagination can be made without pain? Nor will they dream so largely as to affect the world. The elders here do strive to put an end to their offspring's woe. Shield them from the scourge of Napoleon's time. Woe, for the future of imagination will suffer. For grand imagination is born from pain."

Victoria Frankenstein takes a step to the side and in a firm stance rebuts, "No." She speaks with her chin held high and her gaze steady. "Far from it. Mr. Bernardo, that is no way to think. I have seen the offsrping of terrible hearts and minds, therefore condemning their children to a lifelong pain. Those same children with their incurable pain are the figures history is written about. It is with enthusiasm, I say, I am eager to see what will become of a world built from the imagination of kind children. It is the only world we have yet to see."

Bernardo and Victoria look on, watching the children as they take the path back to town. Augusto picks up Madelief and puts her on his shoulders; she lets out a little shriek of excitement as she hangs onto his head. Victoria sympathizes with the connection these children have with each other. A connection kids hold with no intention of severing the ties that bind. An unseen knit made from the yarn of innocence overlaps for them, while they are unknowing of what it feels like to be incomplete without the presence of even one of the children.

Bernardo reaches over to Victoria to hand her a yellow chrysanthemum flower. Victoria takes notice, and with a blush rising in her face, she turns away while reaching to take the flower.

"By my heart, Bernardo. It is with a flustered hand that I receive this token of affection, if indeed that is what you intend."

"Miss Victoria," Bernardo replies, "that is indeed my intention." A small gesture, I admit. Please let it carry the weight of a powerful gesture, for this is all a poor Italian man has to offer."

With a raise of Victoria's hand, she gestures towards the school. "Understand, every school day, Susanna and Madelief travel to the pond in the woods north of town because that is where a batch of chrysanthemums grows. They pick the prettiest ones to gift me, and still, your offered flower has warmed me. Both in my chest and my comfort." Bernardo leans closer, and in a quiet speech, he says, "With winter approaching, I can be trusted whenever you are in need of finding warmth."

An involuntary bashful grin grows across Victoria's face as a shine of pinkness blooms over her lips. "Now that," Victoria declares, "Mr. Bernardo, is most respectful. I intend to take you up on your invitation. When the cold becomes too overbearing."

"I long for the day... amore mio." Quickly, Bernardo straightens up, remembering something. "Ah, yes! Jacop and Geertrudia informed me a feast will be held to celebrate you. What say you, Miss Victoria? May I join in the festivities?"

"Please, Mr. Bernardo. The feast, therefore, would lack being called such if you were not present."

• • • •

LATER THAT EVENING the sound of joyous celebration can be heard within Jacop and Geertrudia's home. Victoria sits to Jacop's right as he claims the head of the long wooden table. A clay pot of soup and a ladle stand in the center, a nearly empty tray of sliced bread, and pitchers of Rhine wine sweating in the lamplight. Guests arrange themselves around plates of fish stripped to the bone. A woven basket holds ragged remnants of cabbage, potatoes, carrots, and dark red beets.

Bernardo perches beside Victoria, picking morsels from his teeth with the easy contentment of a man who has eaten well. Opposite Jacop, Ignaas pours another cup for Wilhelmina, who sits to his left. Geertrudia watches the room with amused eyes, and Knelis sips his wine in companionable silence beside his sister. Conversation threads and overlaps.

Warmth comes not only from bodies gathered close but also from the bright, unselfconscious generosity that shapes the evening. The spirit of these kind people creates an infectious joy. Everyone knows how to focus the celebration on the person being honored. They leave any grudges or anxieties at the door like cloaks, if any at all. For a few hours the household suspends the kingdom's grey horizon. Napoleonic rule hums beyond their reach, a distant, patient storm, but tonight they celebrate survival and the clever genius of Victoria Frankenstein. In the ease of this company, they allow themselves the indulgence of forgetting what looms over their lives and their homeland, if only until the last cup is drained.

Geertrudia speaks up across the laughter of the table at Victoria, "And this is when you were all children? You and Jacop?" Jacop replies, "Yes! Very young children." Victoria has a laugh that is charming and unburdened in this moment. She possesses a sense of freedom, similar to someone who has never experienced the constraints imposed by a controlling person, and even a fearlessness that would prevent such experiences. After she lets out a laugh, she responds, "Yes! Yes, Jacop, we should recognize you were very young. Let that be the defense of the argument for throwing your father's books out of the fourth story window into your mother's garden. Let it also be the defense for your misdeeds against poor Grandfather Roderic."

Jacop deadpan stares at Victoria before grabbing a pitcher of Rhine wine to refill his glass. "Oh heavens. You really do know me too well." Geertrudia questions, "You fulfilled misdeeds on your grandfather?"

"Yes," Jacop replies. "Well, you see, my grandfather Roderic, often in his old age, would be terribly forgetful. Then there came a day wherein, in our library, I was reading with young Victoria, and I could not hold my bladder. Here is my terrible misdeed: I had chosen not to relieve myself in private, but instead I urinated on the library floor."

Victoria speaks up by saying, "Directly behind poor Grandfather Roderic's chair!" Bernardo and Ignaas erupt in laughter. Jacop continues, "When I was finished, Grandfather Roderic, who was too old to move about without assistance, called out to me, *'Jacop, my dear boy... hast thou pissed on thy floor in the library?'* to which I lied by telling him, *'No, Grandfather Roderic. Don't you remember? You did that. Just now.'*"

Wilhelmina lets out a cackle, and Ignaas proceeds to laugh. Knelis spills a bit of his drink as he bursts with amusement.

"Jacop!" Geertrudia exclaims, "How terrible!"

"I was but a child!" He says in his defense. Victoria, laughing, adds, "A very young child... of ten!"

"Jacop!" Geertrudia exclaims again over the laughter at the table. After a moment when the laughter begins to die down, Geertrudia turns to Victoria. "You really have known Jacop since you were children?"

"Since childhood, yes. Jacop's father was my family's financier. My father would take me to see Jacop each day he needed to conduct business, as women were not allowed to receive an education. Women... sorry, women... are... not allowed to have an education in the United Kingdom of Great Britain. I would join Jacop in private tutoring."

"There is more." Jacop says, "Victoria's father insisted on round-the-clock tutoring. She was the disciple to a many educated men. Her father saw to that. She continued taking lessons for hours even after our lessons together had ended. Fencing, as well as sword fighting and hand-to-hand combat from soldiers. She learned from engineers, chemists, natural philosophers, and cultivators of science. She also learned from barber surgeons, who were experts in their respective fields. Medical practitioners, and even a doctor. Teachers from various countries around the world. There is no mind like a Frankenstein's, my father used to say."

"You learned from surgeons?" Geertrudia asks, "That is why you were able to save my sister and her child?"

"Yes, simply put. There is far more depth in my knowledge of the procedure I conducted for your sister. When I was sixteen, my father took me to learn hunting with a Ugandan tribe in Africa. He supplied them with food, seeds, and tools. In exchange they taught us their customs. It was there I learned that when a woman has birthing complications, they perform the procedure to extract the child through the belly. The Ugandan people have been practicing this operation for over two hundred years. In between hunting, I would learn and eventually come to perform the operations alongside the Ugandan women."

"How many women did you save?" Wilhelmina asks. Victoria takes a pause. "How many... women? I saved... two hundred & seventy-seven women. Ambroos is the two hundred & seventy-eighth."

It is only the women at the table who become misty-eyed. Wilhelmina involuntarily has streams run down her face. The table becomes silent, utterly moved.

"But I wish it were more. I returned to the Kingdom of Great

Britain with an ambition to convince the British institutions of medicine to adopt these practices, and they turned me away. They weren't going to listen to a woman, let alone a girl. Behold this zeitgeist of dehumanizing women, for it has stopped us from maturing in medical practices. This procedure would have saved my mother." She says, slightly dropping her head, "My mother passed in my birth."

Victoria stands with all the anxiousness of a slowly erupting geyser. She pulls her hands toward her while sliding her palms across the table. She uses her fingertips to nervously tap at her hips before running her hands down her sides. Jacop leans forward in his seat. "Victoria? What burdens you?"

"This world, Jacop." She answers. "There is a world of knowledge out there, and still the doors are closed to giving this knowledge to the whole of humanity. Simply because it was not a man who came to discover it. I was educated by my father because there is a stronghold on the world, and women are owned, and what is in rule is to deny a woman accessibility to the public streets. Living such a normal life, no different from that of livestock. Goods and wares shelved for fathers and husbands. I feel a deep sense of disgust upon learning that any woman was denied an education. Tutors needed to be accommodated with enough wealth to buy a village in order for me to learn about medicine. Men? The holders of rationale? Where do we discover rational thought when my education came at the cost of a fortune? Only behind closed doors was I allowed to learn for fear the world of men would lay their eyes on a woman with disdain for being equal in their capacity to be rational, self-governing, and powerful. This world constructed a wall of men, standing guard for generations, to prevent women from advancing alongside them as equals. My mother documented the witch hunts that lasted three hundred & sixty years. A phenomenon of accusations and convictions that saw the murder of thousands of women. Imagine if those hands were given the same education as men. How much higher the people of the world would have grown. The world that could have been. The morale that would have grown unhindered in communities everywhere, for there would have been no mourning over the corpses of mothers, daughters, and sisters. The absence of their helping hands has since been felt deeply. The presence of women has been diminished and silenced where, given the opportunity, there would have been seen their contributions to the advancement of this world still in its adolescence. To our disappointment, we now suffer for it, for it is with a pain the body can't recognize that lives in the legacies of slaughtered women. For if ever such a history never came about and a world where the minds of women and men worked together and they raised kind children, then the course of history would find itself in a flourishing direction today. If it were so, medicine would have seen proper hygienic routines and more minds to practice the science of medicine. Then maybe my mother... my mother... may have survived birthing me."

Victoria, with all the eyes of the guests watching her with unbroken attention, thinks to herself, "These people, they will find no reverence in my shunning discussion." And then she says to everyone, "I apologize. I have run away with my thoughts. Please forgive me. Please, do not think me informal; I... I will turn in for the night." She makes her way to the stairs and with her back turned Geertrudia calls her name.

"Victoria! Do not forget, you saved the life of my sister and her child. You see a world without new medicine. For my sister... my kin...

for me. You are the new medicine."

"*I am no good to the world now.*" Victoria thinks. She turns to Geertrudia. "Your compliment is well received, Geertrudia. Thank you for tonight. But I must rest now." Victoria continues up the stairs to her room, where the night of festivities ends for her. She lies awake staring at the dark corner of the ceiling. She gives a withered sigh, fighting back the warm tears of anger and disappointment. "How ungrateful of me," she thinks, "to ruin the celebration with my problems. To call out the world's flaws and how it has wronged the likes of me. I am no better than those I speak ill of, staining the night with my blackened heart. What use am I to the world, old and now indifferent to the efforts of those who truly seek enjoyment in their days? What hospitality could I possibly hope to expect by dawn? Perhaps it would be in everyone's best interest to cast myself out. To spare kind people of an old woman's ramblings." The night grows later as Victoria resolves to leave come morning. Her eyes flutter shut as she drifts to sleep, her heart heavy with the gravity of her emotions.

Chapter 6

The Hope Undeserved

The dim glow of first light fills the room as Victoria sits on her bed, having already gotten dressed before dawn. The silence within the house coincides with her thoughts, and she prepares to tell Jacop and Geertrudia that she will be departing. She plans to head west to Bruges and from there seek work to sustain a room for herself.

She reflects, "My unquiet passions need not bother this town and these people." It's then that she hears commotion downstairs. The sound of movement is quite peculiar, for it is not within the usual hours in which the house becomes alive. Furthermore, the voices do not belong to Susanna, tiny Madelief, or their mother, Geertrudia. It sounds as though a group has gathered downstairs.

Victoria leaves her room to descend the staircase. Only after a few steps can she begin to see that many have gathered in the living room, including Geertrudia, Jacop, and their daughters. The guests have filled the downstairs, leaving many to stand. As Victoria makes her presence known, the room becomes quiet. She refrains from coming off the stairs.

Geertrudia steps to the forefront of the crowd. "Victoria, come... there is much to discuss." She holds her hand out, but Victoria holds her palm up in decline. "I will save you the burden. I am truly sorry to all of you for my outburst. This place is a refuge for the kind, and there was no merit to your witnessing of my passionate squabbles. I have decided to leave. Be a burden to your home and your family no longer."

Jacop steps forward and, in a voice for all to hear, says, "You could not be more wrong, dear friend. It is quite the opposite. There are things I know about you, things you never told me, still I know them. I know you lost a child in the womb in your youth. I know you sold your family's properties, including your childhood home. Furthermore, I am aware that Napoleon's De La Police raided and burned down your ancestral castle. Frankensteins have fallen far from grace."

They both came from a world familiar with high society, where it was common practice to veil your misfortune lest you fall victim to the perception of a weak status. However, in this struggling small village, there is no status to maintain; instead, the community finds common ground through bonding. To know the person who holds the ties that bind them. The gears of Victoria's analytics are turning as she sees this in Jacop's choice to speak of her personal life so openly among everyone. Jacop turns to all in the house and continues, "My old friend, forgive me for speaking out of turn with what you carry, but we all here know burdens. We must carry on in the face of an uncertain world. Even a world we don't agree with. I know the long life you've lived because I have been your friend. I have shared your time. I know what pain you bear. My friend, learn as I have learned, for here you are not alone. See that this can be the last place you call home."

Victoria takes a second look at the faces in the room, and there is no dismay that she can see expressed on them. She has misunderstood the reaction these people are having to her.

Geertrudia steps past Jacop to grab Victoria's hand, and holding it between hers, she explains, "Jacop and I bartered with Bernardo. He owns the vacant house next to his. We took ownership of it. We are giving it to you. We wanted to surprise you last night." Victoria's eyebrows raise high, and her eyes boggle with shock. Geertrudia continues, saying to Victoria, "We want you to stay. You can be a many things. You can be our barber, our midwife, a tiller of science, or the teacher of our children. Be our friend. Be my sister. Let Rode Heuvels be your home now."

The room looks to Victoria, waiting for her to break the silence. Victoria perceives within that she has found a place that has everything one needs. As time goes on, there will be fewer and fewer corners of the world where she feels safe and comfortable. Eventually, time will no longer favor her. A new light paints this world as she sees there are still new moments in this life to find, for she is a woman who has nothing, yet in this moment she has everything. She has come to believe this village is the best example she has seen of a society with kind people raising kind children. She could never have hoped for a better place to settle nor imagined a place where she would be useful at her age. Conflicted still, there lingers a feeling that all this is the work of fiction, wherein she is favored by fortune to be embraced so tremendously. Despite the prosperous opportunity, a heavy cloud of ill weather looms over her that she can't shake off, resembling a hope undeserved.

Victoria then feels little Susanna wrap around her leg. She looks down to see her big eyes staring back. Susanna asks, "Are you leaving me?"

Victoria responds with tears that break the levee, "No. I'm staying." Geertrudia ignites with a holler in celebration, and the rest of the room rejoices in her decision.

• • • •

AS DAYS GO BY, VICTORIA moves furniture into her new home. Most of the furniture, gifts from various friends and villagers, is new and helps her to get settled in. Victoria is a vigorous workhorse for her age. The men and young helpers find that out as they become exhausted quickly, whereas she is energized until the late hours. She employs Ignaas and his blacksmith apprentice, Laurens, to have a few glass decanters and vials made up for her, and in a day or so she will retrieve them when they are ready.

One evening Jacop and Geertrudia walk over to visit Victoria's door to see how she is settling in. Bernardo, using his carpentry skills, made a table to gift to Victoria. After they move it into her house for her, Victoria walks Bernardo out and hears Jacop say with a cheerful laugh, "Death follows Frankensteins, isn't that right?" Victoria looks at

Jacop before closing her eyes, simultaneously giving him a nod.

"To what end have you said this to Victoria?" Geertrudia asks. "My dearest, that is her family motto, part of a larger coat of arms. What are the words, Victoria? Boundless... unbridled power of will... endless..." Victoria interrupts to correct him, "Boundless, unbridled power of will, limitless leornian"

Wagging his finger Jacop nods, "Ah yes! Limitless leornian! Verily, inspiring. You see, '*Death follows Frankensteins*' is their family motto for how they are diligent workers. They work until their muscles burn and never tire until they have reached their goals. They work like death is following them."

"Can I say that when I grow tired yet am still eager to gain?" Geertrudia asks Victoria. Victoria raises her hand out as she responds, "Yes! Please do! I hope it brings you encouragement whenever needed."

Bernardo had stopped to listen, but now he says goodbye and continues on his way home. Jacop and Geertrudia, after a brief conversation, also head up the road for the evening. As Victoria returns inside, she speaks to herself, "He misspoke. Jacop said 'they' and 'them' as though there are more Frankensteins. Thus, he is terribly wrong. Yet my heart becomes too weary to mention, for I am the last Frankenstein. I am the death of my family name."

• • • •

THE FOLLOWING DAY, Victoria arrives at Geertrudia's door to collect freshly picked crops that were promised to her. Lightly knocking, she is then answered by Susanna. Geertrudia can be seen in the kitchen tying up a burlap sack bulky with red mammoth fodder beets. Geertrudia glows with joy as she sees Victoria walking through the house toward her, wearing an open-mouthed smile. It is possible she is more joyous in Victoria's company, but she makes it difficult to tell, as Geertrudia is always blissfully radiant. As she hands Victoria the sack, Susanna dishearteningly asks, "Now that you no longer live with us, does that mean you won't be tucking me in anymore?" Victoria and Geertrudia look at each other and laugh. Geertrudia says to Susanna, "She doth move but a few dwellings away. You shall see her again."

Victoria holds Susanna's hand when she tells her, "I will still come tuck you into bed whenever you'd like."

"Tonight." Susanna chucks out. Victoria finds it all adorable and nods in agreement. "Give me your word." Susanna demands. Victoria kneels down to be eye-to-eye with her, and with a loving smile, she says, "You have my word. Tonight."

When Victoria steps outside, Bernardo joins her in her tasks and accompanies her to Ignaas' blacksmith workshop.

Inside, Laurens, a young Spanish man of nineteen and the eldest son of Kasper and Jacintha, puts four glass decanters in individual burlap sacks so they can be carried without breaking. He is known for his serious, brooding expression and is often focused on the work at hand. Laurens' complexion brightens with his polite smile as he passes the sacks to Victoria. Victoria recalls overhearing Zoe and Yvonne fawning over Laurens, who, with his laborious work, had transformed into a strapping young man with convex muscles and a toned jaw, forfeiting the long and lanky limbs of his adolescence. Victoria could see the love and care that went into raising an astute son. With every visit to Ignaas' shop, she could see the glimmer of pride in Laurens' work as he strengthened his skill.

"I hope your father, Kaspar, is in good health." Victoria comments to Laurens in Spanish. He replies in English, "He has fallen ill this day, not too fierce, yet he is in need of much rest."

As Victoria focuses on the news she has learned, Bernardo gently takes the burlap sacks from her hands.

"Shame. Please give him my best." She says as she leaves.

"Will do, Miss Victoria." Laurens replies.

Upon arriving at Victoria's house, Bernardo places the burlap sacks down. It is then that he becomes curious when he sees a leather-bound journal so unique it screams at him across the room from the desk it rests on. "What is it that you write in there?" Bernardo inquires. She looks up just as he points, and she takes pause.

"What is written in there is the life I had. A time I truly fear to forget."

Bernardo walks over, and as he takes a seat, his lanky, long figure bows at his torso as he presumes, "You were wed."

The fortress she raised, once constructed piece by piece, served to hide her, ensuring that no one would ever see her inner world. But now, she takes the first step in bringing it down.

"I was married once." She replies.

"There must be a devastating reason why you are no longer wed."

"No. The reason for why we are no longer wed was not devastating."

"Then methinks there were no children."

"There was."

"Forgive me, I meant not to speak so impolitely."

"No. It is well that you inquired. I have lost two babes."

"Your babes... They are... What you are afraid of forgetting?"

Victoria looks over at him and smiles with glossy eyes. "That is the first question you've asked about my previous life. You are quite magical, Bernardo, for I've never known anyone to get so many answers out of me without asking a single question." She leans on the wall beside the window. "You are wrong. That is not what I fear forgetting in my journal. And yet, you are also right... I am... afraid. Afraid to forget them. Afraid to forget her. I carry her memory with me, even though she perished in the womb many years ago. I think of her life, moments she never got. I think of the gentle, loving creature she very well could hath been. There were nights I dreamed of her. I dreamed that my little baby came to life again; that it had only been cold and that I rubbed her before the fire and..." She pauses as she stares out the window and slips into a world of thoughts filled with moments that never happened.

Stories she's told herself that began with 'what if.' A little girl who cried for her mother in the dark of the night. A young daughter who wanted more than anything to be just like her. She floats in thoughts of scenarios she has created where her baby stayed here in this life and she watched her grow. In her imagination her daughter grew to be a whimsical Frankenstein, and even that fictional daughter would still have her heart be broken, like all hearts are bound. In these dreamed up moments she held her now grown daughter to comfort her unavoidable pain. She longed for a chance to be the nurturing mother her daughter needed. Hoping for a chance to give her daughter the arms of safety. A feeling of embrace that life never granted her from her mother. Bernardo's voice brings her out of her imagination. "You rubbed her before the fire, and what happened next?"

"...She lived. She was... alive."

"Did you love the babe's father?"

"Thus I felt no hate for that man, but still, to my dismay, there was no love, either. No, I knew true love shortly after my husband and I parted."

"A man who is known by you, Victoria Frankenstein, as the worthy presence of love, is a man who deserved to be named."

"His name. His name was Qansuh."

Qansuh. His name is an oil painting on the canvas of her memories that she returns to refurbish often. The right side of his face is turned toward the late afternoon sun. Light shines through his iris to make the hazel of his eyes appear illuminated, like the floor of a pond that has caught the golds and browns of autumn foliage with water as clear as glass flowing over it.

She turns to Bernardo. "He was a young Egyptian man that worked for my father. Though my father had hired him as an assistant for some years, I, on the other hand, only knew his presence for six months. You must know, though Qansuh was my first true love, I have known love to flourish many times."

"Pray tell, what was the last you've felt of love?" Bernardo explores.

"It has been eight years."

"I see. Wed?"

"Unwed."

"How long was your love?"

"It was the most I've seen of love. It was a love of eighteen years."

"That is a burden on the heart to lose."

"It is."

"If you will permit me to dissect, what was his name? The man you last loved."

"His name was Voivode."

Looking out her window, Victoria sees Benji. A little man, whose face shows the diverse topography created by the stress of labor. He walks into Bernardo's yard. His arms are dehydrated of fat, giving the appearance of his skin shrink wrapped around the formations of his muscles. He has slung over his shoulder a fisherman's coat bundled around boots and other clothing. He glances up to see Victoria watching him, only to peer back with an unwelcoming fixed sneer.

"It seems Benji has returned. He is making haste to your door."

Bernardo gets up from his seat. "I shall behold what tidings Benji bears from his past days. Beloved Victoria, verily I yearn to return and resume our discourse. You are truly worthy of my hours. Never is a moment squandered when it is spent with you."

It is then that they both hear a knock, and Victoria gets up to answer the door to Jacop and Knelis. Bernardo greets them and steps out to return to his home. Jacop has all the calm pleasantness about him as a visitor arriving for a friendly cup of evening tea. Knelis, in comparison, has eyes that move with insecurity and all the confusion of an all-encompassing uncertainty.

Jacop, taking his hat off to her and then returning it to his head, says, "Good evening. 'Tis I and Knelis come to leave firewood and brush." Residing behind the two men is a cart filled with chopped wood and burlap sacks of shrubbery. "I have noticed a frost gently creeping upon my window this morning and in days past. I foresee colder evenings ahead. We shall place firewood here by your door, with a sack of sticks and brushwood for kindling. If ever you need more, call upon us and fear not to be a burden. We wish all a readiness for winter."

"You are saints, Jacop and Knelis. Your work is met with my gratitude." Although Jacop's demeanor remains mostly unchanged as he nods in gratitude to her compliment, Knelis shows a noticeable shift in his anxious behavior; Victoria's words soothe him, revealing a calm and bashful side.

Still standing at her porch, she watches as Jacop and Knelis continue on to other houses. In German, a man can be heard speaking to Victoria from the opposite end of the street, "Good evening, Victoria."

She sees a middle-aged man walking towards her. He strides purposefully as though to chat in passing on his way to other priorities. His hair, a sun-gold blond, is covered with a tweed cap. His build is quite bulky, with all the sculpting of a Greek statue, equipped with bulging shoulders and gigantic hands. Unmistakably, he is the tallest man in town.

"Have you seen Ignaas today? I require his help and worry that his workday has come to an end.

She replies in German, "I have seen him, Albertus. His day of work continues. Fear not. You will find him with his apprentice Laurens in his blacksmith shop."

"You are quite helpful, Victoria! I am grateful for you." He replies, continuing to walk up the street.

Returning inside, she looks over her gift. The handmade wooden table set resides within the kitchen, where pans and mugs hang from an iron frame rack within convenient reach above it. Her desk is in an adjacent room, placed against the wall. The room is an open space with newly built wood-boarded floors and bare lumber beams along the walls. After picking up her journal, she takes a seat at the table. Both of her hands lay over the journal. The journal is bound in leather, completely enclosing the pages and leaving extra space where the spine would typically be. It is bound closed with three ties. A gentle knock is heard, and Victoria calls for them to enter. Bernardo enters and joins her at the table.

"All is well with Benji, I presume."

"Yes," Bernardo responds, "I hear the fishing is bountiful. Do tell." He points to her journal and asks, "Which memory do you revisit from it? I am most eager to hear of it."

"I assure you, the bindings of this journal have not been untied in eight years."

"Forgive one's lack of deduction. I have grown curious, Victoria. Jacop spoke of a family motto of yours. How did it go?"

"Ah, yes. Death... follows Frankensteins."

Bernardo raises his brows. "It is a wondrous strange motto, is it not?"

"Yes," Victoria nods. "Well, you see, my father was born some 38 years after the Frankenstein Lordship was sold. The family branched off, with most finding positions as abbesses, prince-bishops, and canons. So when he fell in love with my mother, a girl who detested the church in all its forms for its grotesque killing of women during the witch trials, he whisked her away to England. She herself was about to suffer the witch trials in Germany, and... he saved her. He started a new life by even going as far as to change his family crest. Thus henceforth, death follows Frankensteins. It was more of a... *'non ti fermare, dai!'* if you will." She says this phrase in Italian, which translates to, "Don't stop! Come on!" Victoria continues, "A moving cause! Words to propel our spirits as a people. To live colossally now, for death is not far."

"What a man of fable. Truly, he merits praise?"

"Indeed, he merits praise. There was no man more blinded by optimism than he. Blindness I inherited. It was one anchor that made him great and was still a terrible flaw in the end."

Bernardo sees she is not easily overrun by her emotion, but still there is a heart that resides within her. Her face cannot hide all the tells of her jaded thoughts. He stands from his seat. "I forgot. I have a surprise for you." He opens the front door and retrieves a bottle of wine he had left outside. "A celebratory drink with me?"

"A marvelous idea. A celebratory drink," she says. After getting two glasses, he opens the wine. A wave of dark Merlot wine crashes in the glasses, and she takes the glass Bernardo offers her from across the table. He raises his glass to toast, "To your new home."

She smiles, charmed. "To my home." They hold a gaze for each other as they respond to the toast with a sip. Her smile grows larger as she breaks the gaze. "There has been so much said of me and so little of you, Bernardo." She says with a blush. Bernardo shakes his head. "There is nothing more I wish to speak of than all things that pertain to you."

Victoria is a fifty-two-year-old woman, and yet in this moment she is blooming with a warmness in her fingers and chest that she thought was a sensation reserved for the young. Maybe there is still a spirit for childlike wonder yet to be seen in these years. It has been so long since she sat down alone at a table as the sky sang with darkening oranges and paint strokes of purple. No pressing matters of any sort currently interrupt two people comfortable in each other's company.

"Please," Bernardo insists, "tell me more of your father. Did you love him?"

"Verily. My father, Johannes Frankenstein, lived charitably. From when the sun rose to its fall, breaths were only taken of his virtues. He stood every day in opposition to society and was still too powerful to be an outcast or ostracized. He walked as though my mother were beside him, making decisions with her perspective at the forefront. Making good on all dealings of my upbringing. The most loving father, truly. It is now, in my old age, that I develop a small resentment for him. How can I say this? I see the spite I have is not for him but for his optimism. For our family crest. Death follows Frankensteins. It should be seen as a warning. Our curse to bear."

Bernardo, pouring himself another glass, says, "That is quite the confession. I believe those are not easy words for an astounding woman such as yourself to permit me to hear. If you may allow, I must confess. I run from a past in Italy I am not proud of."

"Before you is only a woman. No judge nor congregation should submit you to trial. Only a woman."

"A beautiful woman." Bernardo raises his glass once again. "With your best wishes at heart, I do hope you will welcome my compliments."

"Of course. They are welcomed this evening."

"I have a story to tell, one that is filled with shame. In Italy... I have known Benji half my life. We were lucky as young boys to survive. See, we lived like rats in the streets. We took what we wanted. But we took on work as men and began to live a life where we earned what we wanted. Victoria, see, we took, relentlessly we took. Until one day, our coin, our beds, our food... we earned. Verily, earning what we wanted outweighed taking it. Benji grew to be a fine fisherman and a fair trader. One evening he met with an unfair trader. I found Benji in an argument of the uttermost lack of rationale. This man who towered over Benji hits him. And hits him again, again, again. I hit the man to help Benji."

Victoria grabs the Merlot, and while calmly pouring herself a glass, she interrupts, "You killed him."

"I did not mean to, I swear it. This man... I then discover... he is a French soldier in Emperor Napoleon's army. It was the year 1805 when we fled Italy, never to return. That is how we ended up here."

"1805?"

"Yes... have I upset you? I do not speak of my crimes without regret. I simply have no desire to keep anything from you."

"I am not upset. For I too have blood on my hands. Bernardo. Your secrets are safe with me. Grant me the same trust for what I am about to tell you, you must promise me you will never speak of it to anyone."

"You have my word, Victoria."

Victoria adjusts back in her seat while contemplating where to begin. She has a worrisome glint in her eyes as she makes eye contact with Bernardo before speaking up, "In 1805... in the southwest of Germany... a man died. His head was crushed in a water mill. I went against nature to apply natural science and used the variant forms of mutational blood to attempt to resurrect this man back to life."

....

VICTORIA SPENDS SOME time explaining the vivid details of her life's work studying a disease in four subjects over the course of twenty-three years. She tells him about her work, explaining the vial of blood that she injected the corpse with and how it was his revival that led to the events that transpired that night in 1805.

She continues, "People from Mill Valley, the town nearest to the castle, had come to my rescue. They were never to find me; instead, they were met with an unfortunate demise. The dead man was once again given life, but what resided within him was no longer the will of a man. The combination of the diseases in the blood latched to the tissue and was the key ingredient to bring life to a soulless creature. I was foolish not to deduce such an outcome. I eluded the fires and escaped on a rowboat in time. That is when I saw my creature when its unimaginable strength tore my rescuer's limb from limb. Heartbroken and mortified, I took my rowboat across the river. In hopes my creature would not find me. I continued on through the forest around the mountains. Hoping I would journey back to Mill Valley. It would be five days of travel before I reached the town on foot. There was a town no more. The buildings and homes were met with collapse if they weren't reduced to a smoldering pile of black soot. People were pressed into the road lifeless along with the parts of men. I could hear the barking of abandoned dogs and the gnawing of the bearded vultures on the bones of people. The crackling of still-burning fires accompanied my screams. A thought that still bothers me is that there was no one left. No one to bury the bodies. There was no one to tell the horrors. Not a soul was spared. I walked in search of survivors. I walked for only a short time in the carnage, in fear ones juggernaut was still there. I have been eluding my crimes until this day. I never sought Voivode when I left. Thus the fear of leading my creature to him and foreordaining him to the same demise as the town of Mill Valley. 'Twas too unbearable a weight. I abandoned him without a word."

Captivated, Bernardo stares at Victoria as he processes everything. A spark of realization hits him. "And this is your... second babe? A babe, not birthed, but of your... creation?" Bernardo questions.

"Yes." Victoria says, eyes downcast. A twinge of pain as she utters the confirmation. Quickly, a confusion overtakes his moment of triumphantly linking these details, and as he reaches for the wine bottle to pour himself a glass, he asks, "What is this word you are saying? Jugger- jugger?"

"Juggernaut. It is a word that hath been derived from the name of the Hindu god Jagannath. In Dutch, it would be "De Verderver." Bernardo then translates, "The destroyer."

There is a body language she notices, one that lives closely to most of Victoria's expectations of men. There is an unchanged emotion that carries in his voice. A calmness one has when one is unmoved. It shares a place with other men. Men who didn't see her father's name. Men who didn't see her social status. These are men who readily harbor animosity towards her. They despise her for recognizing their own intellect in her. Despise her for being more educated than them. These were men who failed to recognize her as a trustworthy individual. Men who didn't see a truthful person. Men who didn't see a person. Just a woman. "No. Of course," she thinks, "What could a woman say that holds water in a physical world?" She smiles, remembering that unless he has broken from the emergent development this world makes men by, then he is as all men are to act, as though they are cursed to view others as less for their eagerness to be defined as the one true image of a man. They act as if they are on a pedestal, even when they are on the same level or lower than others. They could be dead, six feet below in their coffins, and still believe they are the lion of their domain, where all are less powerful and beneath them. She aims not to be a mirror image of the very thing she despises and chooses quality of spirit over combating personalities, for you can change a man with all the same effort that you can change the wood in a tree. You can either water it and keep it healthy, or deprive it of nutrients and make it sickly. Both would take time and care. Both would be upon one's decision."

"Do you believe me?" She inquires to Bernardo.

"I do." He replies. In her mind, she scrutinizes him and draws comparisons with other men who encounter new information. They become intrigued. They inquire. There is a disposition to disprove existing beliefs or seek more proof to validate them. With Bernardo, she sees none. Possibly he is no more than a product of the world of men. In that world, there is a mindset, "What is there to prove or disprove if it comes from a woman?"

Breaking from the thought, she puts the journal in her hands. "Yes. Well, this is all I have from those times. This journal and " She unties the three laces that have kept the journal sealed. Bernardo watches as a glow projects over his face. Victoria holds up a small glowing vial that was tucked into the leather binding's fold.

Awe comes over Bernardo as he stares in wonder at the light it generates, for it is a kind he never before has known.

"Like a jar of fireflies." He says. The vial produces a blue glow that at its center is a vibrant milky white color.

Gently, Victoria places the vial back in the spine and folds the leather over once again as she says, "It glows as such due to a biological luminescence. There are many animals in the world that have this ability to create light. In mixing all four blood vials together, a chemical reaction caused them to glow. This is the twin to the amalgamation I injected my creature with."

Bernardo is trying to keep himself grounded as he says, unsettled with provoked thoughts, "Victoria, my days are filled with carpentry; I made the chairs we sit in. Your experiment is, if not the most, truly incredible story I've ever come across. You, my dear, are a rarity. I have seen adventure and joy in meeting you. There is so much I wish to learn of you. Curiosity fills me. Pray, tell, what were to happen if someone consumed that vial?"

She raises her brows, put off by the thought. "There is no telling what would happen to the human body if someone were to take this vial into themselves. Possibly become catatonic. Die? Or worse, become a monster. I know it gave life to my creation, but it is now a long forgotten resemblance of what man it used to be, only a shell now for an unstoppable rage. A lumbering creature roaming this world evoking ill will on poor unknown souls."

"I perceive that the unknown must be grim for you," he comments.

"Quite. I am afraid because I know everything about it and the detailed workings of its perfection. I am not afraid of not knowing what it can do but instead that there is nothing that can be done for it has no weaknesses. It carries the amalgamation of four diseases that made their hosts the strongest beings to ever have walked the earth. It is the blood of titans that resides within that one creature. I see now I should not have pursued such a goal to revive life. I won't be the last to do so. It has been with deep reflection that I am aware I squandered time when time was abundant to live within gratitude of my dire time granted with others."

Bernardo replies, "Verily, I am sorry. I know how much you risk speaking from an unbound tongue. In the company of greater authorities for God, you would have been shunned lest they heard you speak blasphemy and prosecuted you even. I assure you my intentions were not to ask questions for the purpose of bringing you anything but frustration. That is farthest from my wishes. You are such a wonder, Victoria. There are few moments in my days when I don't think of you."

"Your words are well received, Bernardo. Understand, I am without the regard of the rest of the world, for I am still so passionate in my words, and I truthfully do not care who hears me. I have seen and felt so much turmoil. I fear nothing about speaking with all of my sharp tongue. It could be anyone; it could even be you who turns me in and convicts me for parading out of society's place to have me prosecuted or quieted. I no longer care. I will speak when I wish, and I will fear no man or law that wishes to make me feel less than a human."

The warm atmosphere of Bernardo's palm covers the back of Victoria's hand that has been resting on the table. She looks at her hand as a natural blush fills her face, and she feels the rough, dry calluses on Bernardo's fingers as he softly slides them into her palm. He leans in merely inches from her face with a longing disposition.

"Bernardo?" spoken softly under her breath. Beginning to breathe heavily, she can feel the warmth of his breath enter her nose and mouth, creating a desire to taste his kiss. She upholds her strength to conceal every indication of the libidinous feelings that are overrunning her.

"Dearest Victoria, never. Never. Never. I have seen your mind conveyed like architecture with every new sentence you speak. Verily, the sound of your voice carries convictions of poetry. You damn your family motto and think far less of your name, but the others are the ones who be right. There is no mind like a Frankenstein's. No woman nor man has done what I have seen you do. There is no assistance I can provide to make you see. For I have never. Never. Beheld such a woman. You are... extraordinary. Therefore, I would much rather take your place for a crime of speaking or blasphemy than turn away knowing this world is losing you. I would give it all for—"

She collides with him, cutting off his last words. She puts her lips to his, with both of their skin radiating a feverish heat. They hold this long, slow press together. Lingering here as those emotions of yearning, wanting, pining, and lust build a flood of endorphins. They kiss and kiss as they stand, and in a vigorous way, they energetically put their hands all over each other like a race with themselves to feel the new places of someone else.

He lifts her onto the table and buries his face into her neck, kissing her fiercely from behind her ear down to her collarbone.

Victoria feels his hands retreat from traveling over her body, and instead they make their efforts to disrobe his trousers. She stops him before he can bare himself. She thinks how this is where she would like their affections to lead to, but she will need more than an evening of conversation and a bottle of wine before allowing anyone to have a getting of her body. She understands that she has aroused both him and herself, but she intends to maintain a slow pace, as this is her comfortable way of allowing her heart to fall in love.

"Dearest Bernardo," she softly says while they both are frozen still. "My intentions are very much to find union with you. Respectfully, I must elude you this evening, not to displease. I would not be the extraordinary woman you speak of if I stopped being a woman of my word. Young Susanna asked of me earlier this day a promise to see her be put to bed... on this evening. I will not break my promise to that child."

She makes her way off the table, maneuvering around Bernardo, who, in his shock, is frozen stiff both in the entirety of his body and the parts of him still covered by trousers.

"I am sorry." Victoria says as she presses out the wrinkled up parts of her skirt. She looks upon his face to then suppress her laughter, for the stone-like way he is reacting is quite humorous to her. She kisses his cheek quickly. "Thank you for understanding." She then makes her way to the front door, and she leaves, saying, "Please, on the morrow, see me whenever possible. I bid you good night... dearest Bernardo." She closes the door, and Bernardo is still standing pressed against the kitchen table with his hands gripping the waistband of his tweed trousers. But now he is alone, as he only loosens up enough to turn his head in complete bewilderment.

• • • •

SOMETIME LATER, VICTORIA is with Susanna on her bed as she brushes Susanna's hair. Susanna, already in her nightgown, acts with discipline in her routine as she sits up straight to make brushing her hair more convenient for Victoria.

"I saw Albertus today!" Susanna exclaims. "Me as well!" Victoria replies. "He is always working on the mill. It is quite rare to see him in town with his mother, Anushka. " Susanna continues, "He is always so kind to me. He says I am the most beautiful girl he's ever seen. My father helped Albertus at the windmill today. I will make windmills for all of the kingdom of the Netherlands when I grow up. I want to make windmills and ships. Truly someday shall I build a grand castle. I will it!"

The mere learning of Susanna's growing vocabulary brings Victoria the purest joy in a way that is like feeling awoken from caffeine as though it is the first time consuming it. She tilts her head back to laugh before saying, "Brilliant child, when did you ever begin to say, 'I will it'?"

"Why, today. I overheard Father say it to Mother. Again, when Laurens spoke to Yvonne. I will it! It is powerful, as it speaks to the spirit of greatness, does it not?"

"So it does, child."

"Yvonne and Laurens look at each other the way my mother and father do. I behold, they are in love. Do you remember the first time you fell in love, Miss Victoria?"

"I do."

"What was it like?"

"What was it like? Hmm... I can still remember it like it was the day before. I can still remember him. His name was Qansuh. I could hear his voice while losing focus of the world around us to journey in his eyes. I can hear the humming bass of his voice, but I am unable to make out his words. Forever, the memory of his voice ignites nostalgia for when I saw him for the first time. Rays of a dying day's sun peered down on him for its remaining moments. The air had no choice but to be still as I felt the tide of his oceanic pull take me in. A gravity coursed through me, pulling me like the magnetic force of two planets inevitably to collide. I could feel it through my heart. It was the booming power of the cosmos, and yet still, it gently whispered to me, "There is nowhere else you are supposed to be but with him." Like my soul knew that I would love him and that I hath only been waiting for him. To love him and be loved by him so much that I want to say his name before I die so that it is the last thing I feel on my lips."

Susanna climbs under her blanket, "So beautiful. I can't wait to be in love." Victoria smiles at Susanna, and it is with the expectancy of a child's eagerness to press forward that Susanna quickly moves on. "Miss Victoria, will you sing me a lullaby?"

"Of course." Victoria answers, laughing off Susanna's nearsighted attention to Victoria's vulnerability as she picks up the candlestick holder by the finger loop. She looks upward as she considers a song. When she recalls a song she used to sing, tears well up in her eyes. One her father had sung to her as a child. She sings:

"May he grow sturdy through my crooning, may he flourish through my crooning! May he put down strong foundations as roots, may he spread branches wide like a sakir plant! May his heart be as pure as a white lotus.

From this you know our whereabouts; among those resplendent apple trees overhanging the river, may someone who passes by reach out his hand, may someone lying there raise his hand. My son, sleep will overtake you, sleep will settle on you.

Sleep come, sleep come, sleep come to my son, sleep hasten to my son! Put to sleep his open eyes, settle your hand upon his sparkling eyes – as for his murmuring tongue, let the murmuring not spoil his sleep.

May he fill your lap with emmer while I sweeten miniature cheeses for you, those cheeses that are the healer of mankind, that are the healer of mankind, and of thy son, the son of a good man.

In my garden, it is the lettuces that I have watered, and among the lettuces it is the world's lettuce that I have chopped. Eat this lettuce!

Through my crooning, appear for him a wife, appear for him a wife, and appear for him a son! May a happy nursemaid chatter with him, may a happy nursemaid aid him!

Through my crooning appear a wife for my son, and may she bear him a son so sweet. May his wife lie in his warm embrace, and may his son lie in his outstretched arms. May his wife be happy with him, and may his son be happy with him. May his young wife be happy in his embrace, and may his son grow vigorously on his gentle knees.

I am restless, troubled, quite silent, gazing at the stars, as the crescent moon shines on my face. Your bones might be arrayed on the wall! The man of the wall might shed tears for you! The mongoose might beat the drums for you! The gecko might gouge its cheeks for you! The fly might gash its lips for you! The lizard might tear out its tongue for you!

May the lullaby make us flourish! May the lullaby make us thrive! When

you flourish, when you thrive, when you labor to the shaking of churns, in your late day find sweet sleep, find the sweet bed my son.
May a wife be your support, and may a son be your fortune. May winnowed grain be your lover, and may the goddess of grain be your aid. May you have an eloquent protective goddess. May you be brought up to a reign of favorable days. May you smile upon festivals.
My son is new born to life, he knows nothing. He does not know the length of his old age. I cry as the crescent moon shines on my face. He does not know the dwelling of the 1000 days.
May you discover, May you eat,
My son, May you be, May you be... good"

Susanna, lying in bed with her eyes wide open, says, "I wish to learn all the words to that song. It is amongst my favorite songs to ever hear. Miss Victoria, My thoughts soar as high as the birds. I have so much I ponder. I have so much to say."

"I am here, Susanna. What is it you wish to mention?"

"There was a man who was one hundred feet tall! He was near the windmill this morning. Methink him a fisherman who has wandered too far from the shore."

"I see, and what clues might have brought you to that conclusion?"

"Well, he was wearing a fisherman's coat and boots."

"I suspect he was nothing more than a fisherman who does dealings with Benji."

Susanna sighs at her answer, "You are right, Miss Victoria. I see things from afar and make a grand story of the little I truly know."

"It's okay, Susanna. G'night to you."

"Miss Victoria? Before you take your leave. You told me of the goddess Beira. You spoke of two names the Scottish called her by. One of them was the Queen of Winter. Pray tell, what is her other name?"

"Well, young Susanna, the echoes of clanging could be heard on the mountainsides from the human skulls she wore on her clothes as they banged together. She wildly rode a speeding white wolf as she raised a hammer made of human flesh. Her winters brought storms and death, claiming lives from all the world. They called her..."

As darkness overtakes the yellow glow on Susanna's face, Victoria smothers the candle's flame and declares, "The Destroyer."

Chapter 7

The Lost Girls

A desk in the schoolhouse displays the fading health of pale yellow chrysanthemum flowers. Victoria stands before the class, starting the day's lesson. This morning was quieter. Susanna and Madelief are not here. No laughter to be heard. No impulsive off-topic comments. Today's lesson is cursive practice. Victoria is sure they are late. The school day ends. Two seats empty all day.

Victoria knocks. Her knuckles clacking against blue paint with urgency. Geertrudia's front door swings open rapidly. "Victoria?!" Geertrudia says unexpectedly, "You knock with distress, sister... Distressed is how you look. What could be the matter?"

It seems there is no need to raise alarm, for Geertrudia's state is calm; therefore, Victoria is certain the girls have simply taken off from school to help their mother at home.

"Forgive me, I am merely curious about the welfare of young Susanna and Madelief, for their absence today at school did not go unnoticed by me." Victoria says with a tone of her worries being quelled.

No words arose. Soon Victoria looks up. She sees the paralyzing confusion that adorns Geertrudia's eyes. "To school they went. You have not seen my girls?" Victoria grabs Geertrudia's hands. "Not this day. In previous days, there were only a few instances of tardiness, yet Susanna and Madelief still arrived. Always."

Geertrudia looks out beyond her door. Peering over the surrounding fields, she speaks in a quiet mutter and asks rhetorically, "My girls are gone?"

• • • •

MOST OF THE VILLAGE is gathered at the entrance around the well. Jacop paces, hands working the air as he converses with Ignaas and Benji. Worry scratches their faces into harder lines. On the fringe, Victoria stands with Geertrudia, her palm a cool, steady pressure as she rubs at her back to comfort her. Bernardo approaches, mud ringing his boots. "What hath transpired?" he asks, his voice low.

"Susanna and Madelief are missing," Victoria answers. "Jacop plans to comb the fields and woods."

Bernardo's jaw sets. "We must do everything." He reaches for her hand. She folds her fingers in his, and lets the touch steady them both. "Do as Jacop bids. They will be found."

Jacop lifts his voice, blunt as a bell. "We search in threes. My wife remains at the well. Victoria, join Benji and Tessa."

His words clamp the moment. She releases Bernardo and pulls Geertrudia into an embrace, promising rescue in a whisper.

Bernardo's face is a page of unread words. Victoria glances back and feels the weight of ten thousand sentences folded into his look. She imagines the pleadings she half hears in the cadence of his breath. For eight years those soft intimacies lay silent; now they stir like coals. She daydreams of words he may say to her in some near future: "You are safe. You are free. I need you, I love you." and then tucks it away. Even as she falls into the rhythm of the search, his gaze follows her, holding onto every second she remains in sight.

Jacop assigns the eastward sweep. "Victoria, Tessa, and Benji will pass the windmill and push into the woods." Jacop instructs as Knelis appears with lamps in a cart, all borrowed from throughout the village, and hands one to each of them. They leave Rode Heuvels in a thin line, across flattened fields, past the slow, turning mill, and under trees that close off sight of what awaits within the woods.

• • • •

IT IS PAST MIDDAY, and the skies are grey and cloudy, but there is still daylight, making the woods easy to navigate. As they comb through the trees, Victoria reminisces about a day back in this last summer that she spent with Susanna and Madelief. That day she unfolded a sheet to lie down near the pond. Eagerly, Susanna and Madelief picked food from a basket Victoria had brought. They sat together near a batch of blooming yellow chrysanthemum flowers. The branches provided the shade, and the breeze gave a fragrance, while the water emitted a chill. They ate, and then they played. Madelief would not go near the water. Her mother taught her plenty of times to avoid it without her near. Every once in a while she would walk near the pond's edge and wag her finger as though to say, "no, no, no."

Eventually the girls played together as Victoria read while lying on the sheet they laid out. With critical thinking running in the background, Victoria strolled over the words in her wilted copy of Mary Wollstonecraft's "A Vindication of the Rights of Woman." She is on chapter 2: The Prevailing Opinion of a Sexual Character Discussed.

She remembers there being a quietness that filled their space in the trees. On that calm day she lowered the book to see Madelief and Susanna had fallen asleep. Holding one another, they found comfort and dozed off in the grass near the sheet.

As Victoria thinks about that day, she smiles to herself, amused to recollect the two girls preferring the grass rather than their picnic sheet.

She speaks up, "There is somewhere I wish to search for them. A pond nearer to the north that they are familiar with. I believe—"

"No." Benji speaks in a deep, growling voice without looking in her direction.

"Benji," Victoria responds with no submission in her voice, "we are here to find the children."

"No, I say, woman!" Once again he keeps facing in the same direction as his next step. Victoria is perturbed with his abrupt aggression and says as she stops walking, "Thank you for acknowledging that I am a woman. How observant of you. Now allow me to acknowledge you for what I observe, child."

He spins around. "What did you say?!"

"Finally, you face me," she says before he gets so close; all she can see is him.

"You will mind your tongue lest you beg to be struck in the name of God, wom—" Victoria brings herself only an inch from his face, where all he can see are her eyes.

"Sir, you have one opportunity to refrain from threatening me yet again. Break your will to do so, and I will show you what I do when I can no longer use my words to resolve a conflict."

He is trembling, infuriated. Tessa watches with amazement how Victoria can stand up for herself with every intention to intimidate and remain calm without so much as furrowing her brow or scowling. In this moment, Benji resembles a rabid dog becoming defensive in the presence of a lion.

"You test me and—" Benji barks, but Victoria speaks over him, "More threats, child?" He glares at her with a paper-thin squint inside his sun-scorched crow's feet.

"Find yourself removed before me, or you will learn why I am without fear. That, sir, is a threat."

Benji flings himself around and continues to walk his previous path. Victoria takes a step forward, about to argue for her suggestion of where to search. Tessa lightly puts her hand on her arm.

"Victoria. I believe we are able to divide to search other places. But if we need more than two people, we would be lacking. Furthermore, suppose we do divide. What if Benji found them? Do we want Benji to uncover the girls by himself?"

It's not a thought Victoria has to spend too much time on, and she replies, "No. I suppose not."

"Very well." Tessa says as she entwines her arm with Victoria's. They walk together step in step. "Victoria? How does one learn to become so... fearless, as you?"

"I suppose, in short. I am not fearless. Simply put, my wishes are behind fear, and I suppose I want more than I am afraid."

"That I am sure of. Miss Victoria. Maybe on our way back we can search where you wanted."

Though Benji stays at a distance, their party remains together even if they are not close to one another. They tread through the Zwin woods. They cross patches where there are clearings in the trees untouched by the world, where the animals have only ever known the deep privacy of its peace. They linger around small puddle-like ponds looking for any signs that the girls were there. Soon they reenter the thick of the trees and bushes. Tessa and Benji noticeably are having difficulty. For them the trees are a struggle to tread through. They are more focused on the obstacles of nature. However, this does not compromise Victoria. Multitasking proves no challenge. Keen are her observation skills as she takes in the vivid details of what she sees and hones in on the sounds of the environment. She is able to maneuver through the woods and effectively search simultaneously.

• • • •

SOME TIME PASSES WHEN they happen upon a shore. Victoria sees the ocean reaching out to a setting sun on the horizon. Black clouds can be seen accumulating. Victoria catches a glimpse of electricity flashing in the clouds. Her voice fights to break through the overwhelming ocean winds. "Is this the Zwin North Sea Coast?" Victoria asks Benji. He ignores her. "Benji. These girls would never come to such a place. Listen to me. They didn't come this far."

He faces her from a distance. After a long pause where he coldly stares at her, he says, "Those girls were simple. I have no doubts they wandered free. Do be expectant as I am. They are no more than foolishly drowned. You will come to see it is what I expect. Without doubt the ocean is the mouth they perished in."

"You believe them dead?" Victoria asks.

"They are only children. You must know they are dead as well."

"I believe no such thing! To believe them simple is only a testament to how little you know them. Truly an ignorant thought. I saw children who—"

"Gab on, you wretched woman." Benji says as he waves her off and continues onto the shore. Victoria screams at Benji, "You will continue by yourself. I know them better, and I am certain they would never have come this far!" She then returns to the woods, westbound. As time passes, she can hear Tessa not far behind.

Soon the dark of night takes over the world.

Victoria is in a part of the woods that is easier to walk through when she decides to stop and light her oil lamp. She can see the light of Tessa and Benji's oil lamps when she looks over her shoulder. The shine of one lamp is noticeably closer.

She enters the clearing her party had passed through earlier. Soon, she is within the confines of trees again, and ahead of her, three lanterns can be seen glowing in the distance. Their lights get closer. As though they stand still. Victoria now sees three people. They hold their lanterns up. It is Pepijn, Kaspar, and Jacintha. As she joins them, they inform her that their terrain was less restricting. They wanted to search more, and their search led them here. Tessa and Benji soon join them.

Benji only speaks to Kasper, "The oil will soon fade, and we will be without light. Let us return while we can still see where we are going." Kaspar and Jacintha look to each other, nodding in agreement.

"Wait." Victoria says. "There is one more place to search—"

"Art thou deaf? The lamp's oil will run dry soon," Benji says, raising his voice at her.

"There is still a pond young Susanna and Madelief were very fond of—"

"We aren't going. Quit with your incessantly trite whims."

"Then return, sir!" Victoria barks, raising her voice to Benji. "Return empty handed and tell Jacop and Geertrudia of your dismissal of their girls' lives. But they have not perished. I will not allow for them to spend even one night, scared and cold, beneath the open sky."

Benji unhesitatingly coils his free hand around his shoulder, preparing to backhand her, "I warned you, woman!" He makes his hand as flat and as stiff as a paddle. But his wrist never leaves such a distance as a foot from his chest. Gripping his arm is Victoria's hand. He wants to swing at her, and when he realizes that won't work, he tries to break free of her hold only to fail at that as well, for now he discovers Victoria outmatches him in strength. Even when he attempts to shove her back She is unaffected by his force. With haste, Kasper steps between them, nudging Benji back in the process. He points at Benji. "There is no need for your violence. Especially toward Miss Victoria, who did nothing to earn it."

Jacintha says to Victoria, "My lady, whatever is the matter?" Victoria replies, "There is a pond. Morning after morning the children visited. One, I have known them to take slumber near. They could be there resting. It is but a chance. But a good chance, I am certain of it."

Kasper joins them. "Let us search this pond. I assure you, the lamps will remain lit. Lead the way. We will join you."

After looking Kasper over for a sign of sincerity, Kasper reads truthfully, and Victoria hesitates not a moment more. She leads the party through the woods. Even Benji follows close behind. The onyx clouds hold reign over the sky, eating the light of the woods to then drown it in the trench of an ocean's deep black. The kindling of their lanterns seemingly fights to illuminate even their foreground. Proving to be a mere dim glow.

As they arrive in the area of the pond, Victoria takes pause to look around for any sign of the girls. Using the weak glow their lanterns emit, the rest of them move forward. Benji is taking hesitant steps. He's going to the pond. The party is now behind him. They continue searching the clearing. He raises his oil lamp. He stops and shudders. There is a man. His figure is large. Broad shoulders wrapped in a fisherman's coat. Black hair parted down the middle with stitches. The man sits at the pond's edge. Benji gets a little closer. He can almost see something. Pale. In each arm he cradles Susanna and Madelief, whose faces harness a pale lifelessness that even the oil lamp's dim glow can convey.

Like a siren blaring with alarm, Victoria, along with the rest of the party, is surprised by the accosting scream that Jacintha bellows out in horror as she discovers the girls are but corpses now. As Kasper and Tessa come to her aid, she cries, "Young Susanna! Young Madelief! No! No!"

"God help us." Kasper exclaims, pulling Jacintha closer.

Benji waves his lamp towards their motionless faces once over and says, "They smell of death."

Victoria sees the side of Madelief's face. She thinks about Madelief's little fingers rubbing the fabric of her skirt with a smile that pinched her eyes shut. She thinks about Susanna jumping under her covers last night, eager to spout about her endless inquiries.

Pale. Pale are their faces. So pale they glow in comparison to the night. Their heads rest within the man's elbows as though he lulled them to sleep. They look peaceful with their eyes closed, wrapped inside his cradle.

A collective weeping emerges from Tessa, Kasper, and Jacintha.

Though it can't be seen, Benji's snarl is so deep it can be heard obscuring his howl as he asks, "Did you commit this monstrosity?" to which a soundless void rounds their senses. A grim song of which there is no melody or tune.

"Sir!" Benji yells, "Why don't you answer me? Have you fallen ill?"

"He asked you a question!" Kasper yells. Benji becomes even more aggressive and screams into the unhearing world, demanding to know, "Who are you, traveler?!" Tell me your name!" to which Benji then kicks him in the back with his heel. For Benji it was like kicking a boulder or a tree stump. As he dissolves into more of a panicked fear, Benji screams again, "Tell me your name!"

Victoria knows its name. She knows that of which magic and nature know its name. Lightning and fire know its name. A conqueror with no pursuit of any monument. A menace for tragedy. The ruling hand of judgment. Death knows its name. It is not tethered to the heart of man. Both its life and its mind are unnatural, having once expired only to be reanimated. It is that as much as artificial. With its one objective intelligence, it will be the folly of man, for it will make not a victory of death but a direction complete.

She thinks to herself, "I know not how to receive it." She has options, but if chosen, they could create moral dilemmas. She could be mistaken, and this is merely a man. If she is right and she is unmoving, she will meet her demise where she stands. To run would be to abandon her party to suffer the unimaginable. She is paralyzed in a web where each thread is its own immaculate colosseum. Some filled with pain and others with fear. A shock to her system as she both processes the death of the girls and also has her heart fill with grave dread.

The man gently sets the bodies of the girls on the ground before him. He then rises slowly. There is a haunting about his shape that brings with it a sense of coming misfortune. Such a monstrous stature that all pleasure of the living resigns and the search party finds themselves deviated from grounded reality.

Summoning every ounce of critical thinking, Victoria's mind is clear with the logic of the undeniable. She knows that this is her creature as it turns around. The lights of the oil lamps run dry, all at once, to show the party only a glimpse of its deceased appearance. The creature appears both hideous and gloomy, with almost translucent dead flesh and ailing black lips. The veil of darkness dictates what can be seen now. The party groans and gasps just as Benji growls out, "MONSTER!"

"The sum of my fears hath found me, and vengeance could not have presented itself more fairly to what I deserve." Victoria contemplates, "The horns of death play for me. I am, as all things in its presence are, meek. Predestined to be doomed as it is just before to burn a perilous path. I see no world contending with its presence. This creature sets a precedent from the tales of Beowulf to the Greek odysseys to the folklore of boogeymen, in which the villains of stories will look to my creature to see defined what the world intends when they say... 'monster.'"

Fierce north winds carry the fragrance of ocean spray and dried leaves. Now drowned is the world in coal-black gloomy terror. Lightning hatefully makes its presence known as though it awoke with anger from a long sleep. With a wild disorder, thunder rings out like war trumpets blown with the passion of blood-filled lungs. The search party trembles like powerless mortals with every bolt that strikes the dirt of the earth, making all of creation shake. The black clouds are impregnated with electricity. With no rain, an electrical storm boils. Just as the light dances above and the woods light up in white flashes for seconds at a time, the dark figure of Victoria's creature begins to glow. A milky white light of bioluminescence ignites from inside its core. It flows through the veins in its chest, into its hands, and around the edges of its face before filling its eyes.

Its still patient energy dies a quick death, and its rage builds with the storm.

It takes hold of Benji, clasping his head between the palms of its hands. A collective gasp is belted out by all, and only when there is an in-between of rolling thunder where the quiet overtakes the night once more, the creature speaks. It stares into Benji's eyes and, with a gaping maw, repeats back to him, "Monster."

Chapter 8

A Traveler Comes

Hot searing anguish writhes in Victoria's eyes as they peer on the scene of her creation. "I bear witness to the giants of nature," she contemplates, "who hath awoken from their heavy slumber to look over us now in velvet black gowns and witness our peril that will dirty the hands of my creature."

Everyone is held hypnotized by the phosphorescent glow of its immortal eyes. They are gripped with stagnation under the world of night and shadows. Explosively, Victoria stretches her hand towards them as the creature takes a firm grip of Benji's head. Simultaneously, in a light, breathless voice, she says, "No."

The creature easily presses its meaty fingertips into Benji's head like it is a soft, rotten fruit and then peels him from head to ribs. Splitting him in two. All anyone can see is the black silhouette of Benji's body. Lightning brings light to the sight of his demise in flashes alone. Victoria beheld the horror of that which was capable of utter destruction. Her quiet breast quivers with whimpering realized terrors. Virtue escapes her while her soul plummets into despair.

She turns and runs. The screams of the others can be heard as they follow in her footsteps. There is now no light left to guide the world in refuge from its coming.

Sprinting in total darkness, Victoria traverses through the trees and maneuvers around the low-hanging branches and shrubs. The path she can remember that leads back to Rode Heuvels is now almost foreign in the chaos and has become one she follows half-blind. Guided only by bangs of light the storm throws around, Victoria resists falling victim to the disarray the animated shadows perform in passing still-frame poses.

The entire world drowned out by the sound of her heartbeat pounding away. It is a grueling half hour of rough terrain where the skirt of her dress is a maddening drawback as it gets snagged on twigs and thorns again and again. In one instance Victoria trips over her undermining skirt, and she plants chest to ground. She curses, feeling the sting from impact. She carries on, reaching the village panting and heaving.

Geertrudia is standing in her kitchen. She stops to listen when she can hear Victoria stammering and hyperventilating long before she explodes through the front door, and when she does, they go to each other. Geertrudia eases Victoria down, with both of them coming to their knees. Her hands, eagerly gripping Victoria's. Geertrudia's tears arrive fast. "What is it? Did you find them? Hath my girls been found? Where are my girls?"

"Geertrudia..." Victoria says sorrowfully through labored breathing. Geertrudia looks her in the eyes in waiting. Maybe there is more, and she would be mistaken to quickly assume something was wrong. After all, she knows in her heart her daughters are coming back. It's only a matter of time... but time goes on as she searches Victoria's eyes for more answers. The answers she wants to find.

"You didn't find them?" She asks with her unbroken stare.

Victoria can feel a warm static fill her face, touching her sinuses, flooding her eyes with tears as she attempts to piece together words, but none escape her lips. Instead, she nods.

"You did?" Geertrudia asks, but there is no need for any more questions. She found all her answers within a single tear that falls fast off Victoria's cheek. Geertrudia's body begins to tremble. A staggered breath is heard just before her cries begin. As if in that final breath, all of her hopes seeped out of her very soul.

The tears soon become uncontrollable, streaming down Victoria's face as Geertrudia collapses into her in a realm of grief. They cling to one another as though the world is falling apart, staining each other with heavy tears.

While coddling her, Victoria says, "There is a man. They will call him a traveler. The traveler descends upon us. Geertrudia... He is not a man. Its nature and its name are the one true destruction. Its strength, measureless. A vanquish foreseeable, impossible." Geertrudia retreats from her lament, focusing on Victoria speaking. "It marches a grave path with no human desires but to be a device of wrath."

Geertrudia grips Victoria by the shoulders. "Your claims are ones of paramount. Your conviction is true, but maybe the night makes illusions to cheat your eyes?"

"No..." Victoria responds with conviction. "Do not doubt this truth, Geertrudia. It is a creature of unrest. We must seek refuge while there is still time. All earthly hopes are vain. The destroyer comes to retrieve my soul."

Geertrudia pauses. She lets go of Victoria suddenly, her hands idling briefly while looking away in contemplation. She looks back and then stares long into the deep recesses of Victoria, where she keeps the tells of her truths.

Victoria hesitates to speak as she sees a thought grow behind Geertrudia's eyes. In an instant, Geertrudia's face changes to hardness. A distant coldness rests on her features, misplaced in her usually warm and joyous face, and then she asks, "Why does the traveler come for you, Victoria?"

Victoria takes her time to respond, all the while with shame on her face. It was only a matter of time, as she hid her despair less and less, and she knew as she let it out that it would be the coming of her unveiling. The very revealing of her own dire secret. There is no hiding now what she knows she is.

"It comes for me because I am the guilty maker of that creature. One's claims of paramount ring true. I restored a man's life through the application of natural science in a lab that only high society could afford. The life that was returned was that of a hollow soul, who only wishes to vex me as inferior."

Muffled sounds of commotion come from outside. Men yelling in a heightened urgency. Victoria and Geertrudia both turn to listen in. Faint screams can be heard penetrating the walls. The indistinguishable voice becomes clear when Kasper starts to yell, "A traveler comes! He killed the children! The children, Susanna and Madelief! He killed Benji! With! His! Bare hands! Quickly! Arm yourselves with a weapon. The traveler comes!"

Geertrudia stands up. She almost takes a step but changes her mind and remains standing over Victoria. "I stress to comprehend you. I don't believe you liable in cruelty."

"Geertrudia, nor should I ask of you to comprehend such a profound story. But my words ring true. I arranged the parts of multiple people compiling a puzzle of human pieces to make a dead man live again. Instead I created a monster."

Geertrudia says, holding back tears while peering down on Victoria, "Did my Susanna... my Madelief... meet their fate at the hands... of... the traveler?"

Victoria weeps, "You would be right."

"Your monster, one and the same?" Geertrudia asks in scorn.

"... You... would be right."

"You have taken a hand in their presence?"

"Geertrudia, hear my plea, we must go before it arrives."

"Tell me, Victoria. You have taken a hand in their presence?" She asks again, weak and softly, with her crying eyes shut.

"I did not know they would find me... Yes. I take hand in their presence."

Geertrudia walks to the front door, and Victoria reaches out to her,

"Geertrudia, please—"

But Geertrudia doesn't stop till she reaches the door and refuses to turn around as she says, "All of your right. All of your good. My girls entrusted within you. It was your misdeeds that brought about their demise. It was you. The good I longed for in this world was in my girls. Now they are gone. I couldn't be their mother, for what a mother is meant to do for her daughters. For any illness or mortal wound, I would have given my life in their stead. Anything to protect them, but I did not foresee this. I couldn't protect them from this fate. A fate you claim now to have brought upon them. My heart for sisterly affection, I now cast into the fire... to burn."

It is with anguish and inconsolable pain that Victoria shutters upon hearing this, to then coil into herself, whimpering. Geertrudia continues outside, grabbing an axe along the way. With eager determination, Geertrudia joins Jacop, Knelis, Kasper, Ignaas, and Laurens, who are wielding pitchforks and axes. They all crowd the entrance to the village.

"This is no man, but a destroyer!" Victoria screams as she steps outside. A scream that halts everyone in their tracks. They turn their heads in her direction. She then screams in a fury that carries through the village. With everyone alerted, she yells out, "We must flee while there is still time lest we are to face imminent peril. Not a one of your weapons can do anything to harm it. The same force that gives the storm over us its power grants this traveler its unyielding nature. Deathless is their will. They mock pain. It may very well prove to conquer time. You cannot judge my legible words. It brings a rampancy, worst of all ways yet, if worse there any. It will uproot the surface of the earth and grind you into a clay beneath its feet! Scorching all it crosses, it will put out the fires with your blood. There may still be time! Heed warning now! Will no one listen to me?! It will destroy everything!"

A menacing march echoes in the darkness of the fields before Rode Heuvels' entrance. All who are present hear it and turn to stare in awe. Prowling in the dark, the creature's veins and eyes glow as it descends on the village. Light that flashes in the clouds steals the blackness it lurks in to reveal its massive figure.

"My eyes deceive me." Laurens says.

"He is one hundred feet tall!" Jacop belts out. Under her breath Victoria says, "It's too late."

Along with them all, Geertrudia sees the glow the traveler emits and then turns back to Victoria with a look of sheer terror stressing her face. They lock eyes. Victoria is far from redeeming herself because the bond they once shared has been broken. There is no time or apology that could ever mend the hurt of the indirect betrayal Geertrudia experiences. But right now, she could do right by Geertrudia. Right now they need each other. Maybe together they can be stronger. Geertrudia needs her in this fight, and she shoots a look, gesturing for Victoria to look behind her. Victoria turns around. Another axe. It rests beside the front door. Quickly she wields it with both hands and joins Geertrudia's side. They brace themselves. The time to run is gone. For Victoria, the past has arrived.

Now just outside the entrance to Rode Heuvels, the electrical storm's wrath grows. Bolts of lightning spear the ground around the traveler. A humanoid conduit, enthroned with lightning in the realm of gloom. Fear can be felt coming from the earth as thunder appears to ring out from whence it stood. Victoria and the others appear as sheep served up to slaughter. Pitiful little things for it to annihilate as it is made to meet the futile scorn of vengeful men. The stars have fallen from the sky as though they hide from sight, choosing not to bear witness to what misfortune is to come, taking mourning in silent suffering. Geertrudia stares as though she doesn't look upon a man but more that of a ghost. The lumbering of the dead risen. She peers into the impossible and faces its storm stupidly with having bravery shriveled up on her. She blurts out in a frightened tone loud enough for Victoria to shiver when hearing her say in Dutch, "De Verderver."

Chapter 9

Victoria's Juggernaut

Victoria reflects on her time in India, for that is where she learned about the Hindu god of all creation. Jagannath. Upon British integration into India, the name was received as more than that of just creation but that of the mighty and all-powerful mover. Jagannath was revered as a god capable of destroying everything. A god of annihilation. A truly merciless force that would be... unstoppable. The name transitioned in the integration to "Juggernaut." A formidable, perilous force.

The storm, an unruly chorus of lightning and thunder. The bolts, sharp as the breakaway limbs of century-old oaks. The wind whips, and the cold of it lashes at Victoria. She can see a blueprint, the pieces of all the factors in this gallant stand, and they are more than unprepared. The odds are building up against them. It is only a matter of time before the cold will cut through their clothes. Their weapons have a fortitude that will eventually fail. Exhaustion is not far after combing the fields and woods half the day. She feels hopeless taking a chance on a losing gamble.

The axe in her hands is of no significant matter. She feels weaponless still, and it reminds her of how she felt when she was taught how to hunt in Zimbabwe at fourteen. It is a specific memory of when she had only a spear, hiding among the grass to stalk oblivious antelope. In that time she was unaware she was being hunted by a Barbary lion.

The grass folded under each calm footstep behind her, while the deep rumbles of the lion hummed like ripples in the ground. A prowling quake The musk from his mane carried in the air, giving him away to his prey.

It was strong within her to act carelessly and at the same time confidently. She spun around to face him, meeting him eye to eye in the walls of the tall grass. Raising her spear perfectly between them. He may get his kill, but so would she. If the crushing jaws of a lion were to be her death, then she intended to face it without the anger of a fearful dog or the groveling of a rodent. She was afraid but was still terribly oblivious to pain at her young age. She almost could spare a bit of humor to think that death itself would indeed need to see her out with a Barbary lion.

"For I am, the Victoria Frankenstein. The greatest of all animals is needed to bring about my fall."

Tearing through the air, the lion's massive paw takes her spear, leaving her weaponless. She held her calm demeanor, staying strong with confidence in the face of diversity. He growled and roared, attempting to make a crack in her strength. He then searched her for any signs of weakness. Maybe he saw in her a lioness. Perhaps she was not sufficient to satisfy his hunger. Maybe he knew Victoria, not as a beast nor human but as another, and he chose on his own accord to leave her be that day but not without a long, curious look at a rare species. She contemplated being torn muscle from bone, piece by piece, and knew death was a moment away. She then began repeating in her head over and over as she stared into his eyes, "Death follows Frankensteins."

Far from those years now, Victoria can feel the night air biting and hear the lightning's growl echo high above. It is with unquestionable fear that Victoria feels weaponless again; now traveling with a lifetime's knowledge of pain, she is burdened with doubts of victory as she faces a great beast once more.

"Death has followed this Frankenstein, and it has finally arrived to put an end to us once and for all." That is not the only thing within her thoughts that she has no doubts about.

She is certain that there is no heartless cold this creature could suffer from, for it will eat the fortitude of any man-made weapon. It knows no such boundary as exhaustion. It is the artificial human that will prevail where mankind will fail.

No credit to the ghostly wind that passes through Victoria, but instead all merit goes to the fear that rises like a tidal wave. It's the way there are no oil lamps or torches present, but the burning light coming from her creature's arteries that make the darkness bright. She sees its pale dead flesh is drowned out by its ultraviolet glow, and she tries to look past the terror of the worst of shadows and light that she beholds.

Lightning cleaves the sky as a titan strides forth. It stands like a ruined cathedral of flesh. Limbs that have been roughly shaped in cruel geometry, shoulders spanning like fallen buttresses. Nearly eight feet tall, its hair hangs in fetid black ropes. Even night's cloak cannot swallow the way its eyes pulse white, and in each flash a blade of lightning echoed from the storm.

It moves with awful deliberation. Each step a seismic event that shakes the brumal dirt. As if the very earth fears the coming of doom. There is a terrible, practiced readiness about it, yet its shape is grotesque, as if humanity has been folded and distorted around a monstrous core. It wears a fisher's coat, overalls, and boots caked with sea salt and mud that have walked the ocean's graveyard. The garment should anchor it to the ordinary, and instead it makes the creature obscene, a familiar thing made monstrous. The world leans back from its approach.

More lightning relentlessly rips the sky like a verdict. The creature crosses into the village. Its outline, a black maw. A hulking mass moving with the inexorable slowness of a tide. The stark, unforgiving light strips the seven of any heroic aura. Instead of seeming grand, they appear fragile and vulnerable, like paper-thin mortals at the village entrance.

The seven press close together to choke its path. Breath clouding. Hands white on handles that feel suddenly childish and small. Pitchforks and axes whose edge has never tasted blood. Geertrudia and

Jacop mutter prayers like a stammering charm, the words snagging on the storm. The wind steals their syllables and tosses them into the dark.

The creature's steps do not hurry. A head bowed as if in a census of ruin. Silence becomes a living thing between heartbeats. The villagers can feel the time thicken. A long, suspended moment in which courage might be measured and found wanting. Then the monster lifts its head. Its eyes are white and patient and absolutely sure. The seven tighten their grip at the sight of it. Whatever happens next will be measured not in seconds but in the weight of those lifting eyes.

Eight years passed, on a similarly dreary night when lightning chased away hope and darkness was broken by that creature's abysmal glow that was clawing its way out.

Victoria feels she is rescinding within herself, confronting the sum of all her fears. It is disheartening for her to witness the valor of those around her eroding and cracking as they experience this level of fear for the first time, caused by a monster unlike any the world has ever seen. Involuntarily she remembers the sights of that day eight years ago when she walked through Mill Valley. Where she bore witness to the aftermath of her monster's destruction. The sounds of animals picking apart remnants of flesh echo in her mind still. A preview, perhaps, of what's to come, for she has brought the scorn of nature unto this village and the lives of its people.

With a blinding white flash and an earth-shattering crack of thunder, the monster's lantern eyes swivel. Making an election for extinction, they fix on Knelis. The already timid Knelis stands even smaller beneath that terrible focus. Slack-jawed, a ship drawn to a lighthouse beacon soon to wreck. The thing is not merely large; it demands the forsaking of all hope, for it is an incarnation of oblivion. The juggernaut destined to unmake men. Knelis is a porcelain figure before a mountain of deliberate calamity.

Bolts split dark heavens. The behemoth lunges, more shadow than body, a ghostly blur of power. Knelis thrusts his pitchfork. The handle snaps like old bone, splintering. The creature clamps onto Knelis' wrist. Its fingers close like iron clamps, twisting the very marrow. Knelis' agonizing cry follows, a cry raw with torture, only to be swallowed by the roaring wind. Lightning bleaches the scene, and for an instant, blood, like black water, streams over Knelis as he is lifted off the ground and dangled, a hunter showing off their wounded catch.

Then the monster hurls him. Knelis whips through the air and slams into a house. The impact is brutal and absurd. He bangs against the exterior before collapsing to the ground, limp.

The six others brace. Their faces are pinched and raw. "Keep it from the village!" Jacop barks, his voice a snapped wire. They form a ring, weapons clutched like last hopes, and still they all can't help but feel what they wield has been devalued to useless tools. The colossus advances, and their resistance snaps and reforms around it. Each swing of an axe or thrust of a fork meets air or iron. The tools are glimmering in the monster's illumination. Its arms move with the inexorable force of wrecking beams, sweeping in balletic, lethal arcs that send their weapons skittering.

Time compresses into bright, stuttering instants. A lightning flash catches the juggernaut's fist as it descends toward Victoria. She meets it with her axe. It is like metal kissing metal, and sparks scatter like malevolent stars across the churned ground.

"We must put him down!" Jacop roars. "Kill it! Kill it!" Ignaas growls his assent as their pitchforks and axes maneuver wildly. One by one, they all counter with fierce valor.

Victoria, nimble, is a blade of motion. With eyes aflame and her stony resolve set against the torrent, she sidesteps a crushing blow. It is one she answers with a clean, practiced swing. Steel bites hide, but the monster does not falter. Each strike glances off as if hitting weathered armor. The creature's hide takes and returns thunder. Its inner light swells, making the night itself seem to pulse inside its skin. Even as the juggernaut's overwhelming strength threatens to reduce each defender to sorrowful fragments, their determination is a valorously inspiring spirit.

They press on. Each clash is the ringing of metal, the wet squelch of flesh, and the storm's percussion sowing them together. But the task soon exhausts most of them. Muscles slacken, breaths shorten, and courage thins into stubbornness. The storm is an orchestra. Each strike aligns with the tempo; wallowing of deep grief for the courage in the courageous is dwindling in the face of unstoppable doom. The crescendo arrives. When the colossus raises both arms for a sweeping, obliterating arc, all six synchronize into a single instinct; to retreat in unison, dodging backward beneath the shadow of annihilation.

Victoria sees everyone's exhaustion and, with a firm decision, yells, "Our efforts are futile. I will run and retrieve a horse. We can attempt to drag it out of the village!" she declares in a strained voice.

"Quickly go! Get two, if Pepijn can be found. We need more men!" cried Jacop, voice raw with desperation. It is then with that command that Victoria darts through the village.

In the maelstrom, every lightning flash revealed the harsh anguish in Kasper's overexerted eyes and Geertrudia's fatigued pleas. Each of them soon continued in combat, sinking in the juggernaut's monstrous symphony of violence. It is cleaving through their fragile hope as if it were nothing more than the cloth of their once Dutch Republic flag, ripped apart by Napoleon's Grande Armée during their occupation.

Victoria is sprinting through the village's dirt streets. When she reaches the stables, she finds Pepijn inside. Wasting no time, she moves frantically, void of hesitation in her movement as she prepares a horse for her to take. All the while she is yelling at Pepijn in Dutch, telling him to follow her with rope and a horse. Victoria makes a lasso of their ropes, then they mount their horses and leave the stables together, riding through the village.

• • • •

AT THE TEMPESTUOUS entrance, the melee surges with agonizing cries. Laurens' muscles burn with effort as he jabs twice with his pitchfork, only to be pulled in close by the creature. In the ensuing chaos, Laurens is struck so violently that he is lifted off his feet, crashing into Geertrudia, whose head rebounds cruelly against the ground, leaving her unconscious. Amid the pandemonium, Kasper hears galloping hooves in contest with the wind and turns for only a second to catch sight of Victoria and Pepijn, approaching on horseback. A brief flicker of relief. Reinforcements have arrived. Only to then be snatched. Hands closed like a trap.

Before anyone can move, the monster's fingers engulf Kasper. It lifts him as if he were no heavier than a sack, hoisting him high into the lightning-raked air. Voices shred the storm.

"Put him down!"

"Let him go!"

But there is no convincing it to change its course of action. It regards the cries as background noise.

Then the violence is surgical. It folds Kasper in half. His bones protest with one quick, crystalline note. Victoria screams, tearing vocal cords, "No!" Pepijn's horse won't go any further as he pulls back on the reins, but Victoria races forward.

It folds him again, with the same effortless creasing. Kasper's body is a broken shape. Squeezed into submitting a wet, final breath.

The monster drops Kasper at its boot with a dull, casual thud. Adding punctuation to the creature's discard of him, effortless and unwarranted of notice, as if it dropped a stone. Kasper's body lies there. It is obscene in how completely it is finished. All hold in a silence where even the wind seems ashamed to move.

Lassoing a rope, Victoria ensnares the creature's neck, and leaping from her mounting steed, she then quickly and aggressively smacks their hide. Her juggernaut is briefly toppled, pulled off of its feet as the galloping horse tears free into the fields, dragging the monster in their tracks.

With four still standing, they rally once more. Jacop seethes with anger. Pepijn dismounts with a rugged urgency from the other side of a weathered well.

But using only its hands, the monster quickly tears the rope off. Standing just as lightning strikes, its carnage spooling. Soldiering through the night, it draws near to face them again with a grim determination.

"Impossible!" Jacop barks. Pepijn tosses a bundle of ropes over to Jacop, and as the monster returns, Pepijn is quick to throw his lasso, ensnaring its arm. Jacop quickly throws his lasso, and it catches around the creature's neck.

Temperatures only get lower. Jacop and Pepijn's hands are chapped and sore in the freezing air as they pull at their ropes with every last vestige of strength. The rogue threads in the ropes are stinging needles. Still they pull, and it makes the skin beside their fingernails crack and bleed. Ignaas joins Pepijn and grabs the rope to help him pull. However, he feels disheartened by the realization that three men cannot compete with this creature. He can see Laurens as he regains consciousness.

"Laurens, run!" Ignaas screams, "Find Albertus! We need him! Check the mill! Hurry!" His voice imbued with the weight of despair. Laurens scrambles to his feet to flee, kicking dirt about as he goes.

Pepijn starts yelling in Dutch with non-stop curses and questions, and Ignaas is doing his best to reply while struggling to keep the rope anchored. The relentless assault of the creature drives fear into all their hearts. Its aura, for all to see, is a hostile light rivaling the brilliance of the storm, as hostile a light as the lightning that cracks. With each thunderous boom, the men shiver. The light the monster emits seems to be claiming every ounce of hope. It is an unforeseeable victory, for how must they prevail with their strength fading, but the monster's is insurmountable?

An axe rests on the ground. Victoria grips the handle and wields it once more. Then, the rope snaps taut like a wire. The monster plucks it with effortless amusement. Pepijn and Ignaas are taken off their feet. Their bodies launch toward the monster.

In one motion, the creature raises its arms and then slams down on Pepijn. His body meets the blow mid-air. Inertia flips into ruin. He slams into the ground in a sound that is more collapse than impact. Lying motionless in a crumpled mound. His body asunder. The monster kicks Pepijn in the ribs with a force that heaves him at the mouth of the well. He gets caught under the well's roof and slips inside. Pepijn disappears behind the bricks, falling down into its depths.

After Ignaas hits the ground, Jacop stumbles over with a frustrated clumsiness. He pulls at Ignaas to help him come to his feet, but Ignaas struggles with being battered and bewildered.

Ignaas looks behind Jacop to see the monster rise to its full stature. Within, he is exhausted and rationalizes that there was never going to be an opportunity where he was faster or stronger than this creature. It was never far behind, and it was frightening to feel that the greatest desideratum of the monster is to have utter decimation pass through its hands.

Jacop turns around, and the two men watch in awe at the speed at which the monster runs towards them. Their guts liquefy and their eyes bulge, for the sight of it takes them to a place beyond fear. A place that lives in the twilight of just before hopelessness. It is the dying of resilience.

Suddenly, Victoria's lasso finds purchase on the creature's ankle. The sharp slap of Pepijn's horse's hide resounds as the monster staggers, its feet buckling beneath the force and pulled out from under it. Pepijn's horse runs off with the rope tied to its saddle, and the monster is dragged along the grit. As the monster passes Victoria, she raises an axe above her head.

At that moment Geertrudia's eyes flutter open in a haze of pain, and she watches as Victoria swings her axe at the monster with the same fury as lightning, the cold steel biting into flesh with a hiss as it hits the side of its face, barely causing injury.

As it is dragged away, Jacop brings Geertrudia to her feet. Jacop, clutching Geertrudia's arms, pleads, "Run. Running is the only way to survive."

"No!" she argues. "There is nowhere for me to run if you are not beside me!"

He begs her, "Nor is there a life I want without you! Please, love. Run!" The relentless, punishing roar of the storm drowns out their voices, even as she protests and refuses to abandon him.

Just then screaming lightning rains down in a barrage of explosive booms. Victoria can see the light of the monster moving astoundingly fast, barreling through the night in a path destined for them. It surges forward with a speed that defies belief. Picking up a pitchfork and dashing, Victoria runs to collide with her monster. Attacking with fierce abandon. A pitchfork clenched in her quaking hands cuts through the heavy air as she drives it into her monster's gut upon collision. As the prongs pierce it, Victoria takes a second to smile at the wound. But her victory is short-lived.

Taking control of the pitchfork, the monster dislodges the prongs, and with Victoria still holding on, it throws her. She lands on the other side of the well, skidding across the ground.

"Help Victoria." Jacop commands Geertrudia. He then runs to pick up one of the axes.

Geertrudia goes to a disoriented Victoria. She jerks at her arm with a cruel force. There is a panic in her hands that doesn't hide a clear disregard to treat Victoria tenderly. Eventually Victoria stands, and they both see Jacop and Ignaas attacking the monster. Their will to fight is there, but both men look pathetic. The monster is aggressive and erratic as it emits its cold glow in the pitch black.

A moment of opportunity arises. The monster swipes at Jacop, leaning over too far, and it misses.

Jacop's eyes widen in knowing what he must do. With both hands, Jacop swings his axe overhead. The monster, unable to reset fast enough, is twisted in itself. The edge of the axe blade comes down and cuts into the monster for the first time. Metal edge disappearing into its neck. Milky white ultraviolet pours out. The creature's head bows when it drops to its knees. Blood that glows fountains out of the wound. Neon rivers spill and gush as the titan sits, slumped over. There is a still atmosphere as the intensity of the fight abruptly stops.

The watching storm flickers while Victoria searches for those beaming white eyes. She knows it can be slowed down. But it cannot be stopped. Whatever happens next will be measured by those lifting eyes. Then the monster lifts its head. Its eyes were glowing white and absolutely sure.

Jacop is immediately accosted with the monster's unrelenting nature as he is struck. In shock, he looks down to see the monster has gouged into his stomach with its hand. Its knuckles swimming beneath his organs.

Geertrudia falls to her knees screaming animalistically, while Victoria is catatonic and mortified. The air is stolen from her lungs. As though she has been pierced herself.

Jacop looks upon that baleful light bursting from the creature's body that resembles tree roots. The glow comes from within its hands and wrists. From under the coat it wears, its veins run out from its chest and up its neck, hugging the monster's face. Its face, mountainous and leathery, like any man who has been hardened by laborious toil. He is forced to stare at its eyes that burn bright with a white fire.

The monster quickly stands, lifting Jacop with it. The monster's hand drills through his stomach.

Jacop's eyes mirror the reflection of the lightning that arcs overhead, backlighting the monster's arm as it pulls back, blood trailing in an arch when it destructively erupts out of Jacop's sternum. His body is silhouetted before the monster's shining presence. These dark hours steal the color from sight, leaving a shadow dance of what is made feasible of Jacop's mutilation. He drops to his back, unmoving.

With a pitchfork, Ignaas hits the monster in the back. It's worn down, bent, and dulling at the tips.

The monster turns around, swinging wildly, and with each treacherous step, it comes for Ignaas, motivated. Ignaas runs for his blacksmith workshop, to which the monster sprints after him. Ignaas throws the pitchfork aside, and upon entering his workshop, he seizes a metal rod, a piece of scrap metal that was sitting in a large wooden bucket of water. The bucket's rope handle is hoisted on a hook. Ignaas dips the dry end of the rod into the furnace, where a resting batch of molten metal is still glowing with red embers in a pool of burning yellow.

The monster close behind makes a mad dash into the cramped workshop, filling up the space with its size. Ignaas sees his mistake all too late in luring such a creature of grand scale in here. The monster rushes to Ignaas, taking the brunt of the rod's molten tip before pummeling him across the workshop. He crashes into the dangerously sharp metals and hooks, colliding with the bucket of cooling water. The rope handle on the bucket breaks, spilling the water straight into the furnace's molten metal.

A geyser of golden fire and smoke explodes through the roof of the workshop. It raids over the roof and other nearby houses. Countless sparks and embers are carried by the wind. The workshop catches fire and quickly is brimming with a vicious inferno. Victoria and Geertrudia raise their arms to shield themselves from the flash of heat. Victoria gazes into the fire, feeling the world she cherishes tearing away, one fragile piece at a time, within her soul. She thinks, "My juggernaut will destroy everything. Nothing will be left standing against the overwhelming tide of its power."

Geertrudia gets up and in a coarse voice says, "God help us." She stands in the anguishing winds that batter the village. Her wooden clogs are jagged and cracked with embedded rocks. Ignaas' blacksmith workshop, one of the cornerstones of Rode Heuvels, now breathes crimson tongues of flame. Wind-tossed hair whips across her eyes, rimmed in dirt and tears. Through the heated haze, she sees the corner of the workshop collapse into glowing embers, and though her voice is faint under the storm, her weeping shatters the night.

Victoria's feelings boil, and her personal animosity spills within her thoughts. "There is no God in it. The tyrannical creation. That titan I've awakened brings foreseeable ends to all the places in the world that have found peace. There are nightmares I wish to return to that never reached the heights of terror where my heart endured exhausting torture. Nightmares that held a better place than this one. Where I have cried. Cried in sorrow to the end of tears and cries, and still wallowed more. A peaceless life, where no meal or silent rumination is safe from the stains of horror this monster has made me to see. I wish this pain on them, in hopes there is some lesson they will learn, a mental stone turned to the face of empathy and a relearning of love, and the love of humanizing the people of the world. To see people as beautiful again the way we see nature as beautiful. The way we stop breathing to watch a single dewdrop on a tulip's petal in spring or the way the clouds build like castles in the sky high above the mountain. Still, to see them as people is enough, as a body of dreams, worlds residing under the surface housing compassion's, loves, fears, needs, and talents. Still ill, I am confident in my clairvoyance and predict such a measure would be... it would be... to no avail. For, to be a monster, it would first mean eradicating all remorse. There is no heart to seek out, none to negotiate with. I see a profoundness in perpetuating the belief of God now. To believe there is an all-loving entity, and yet it is always the remorseless, unempathetic, dehumanizing, bloodlust monsters that

"God" grants power to. It is power, the pursuit of it, and the abuse of it that have killed God the swiftest for me. I hope to climb above the pillars so that I may spit in the face of such a maker for the cruelty of their negligence."

Chapter 10

In Destruction's Wake

In her perilous run, Geertrudia is a banshee wailing with a grief that haunts the soul as she goes to Jacop. The fires rage, and the light rises and falls as she slides across the ground. She pours out sorrowful tears before Jacop. The face of his torso is splayed open, exposing the torn flesh and muscle beneath. His bare heart glistens from the fire. Still intact, it beats rapidly, but what consciousness there may be in Jacop has given way to shock.

"Jacop," she cries. "Jacop, no." Her voice now speaking with softer words. Geertrudia stares in his eyes with denial in her heart and draws a caress along his face, "Love. My Jacop." All the while Victoria has come to stand behind her. They see his heart beat slower. Eventually coming to a stop. Mourning consumes them both. Giving her arm a tug, Victoria gently and slowly implies it's their time to depart. They must get up. They must go. They need to go. Her implications become more forceful as Geertrudia remains unmoving over Jacop's dead body. They need to go now. "Geertrudia," Victoria says through tears, "we need to run."

Finally she is able to pull Geertrudia away despite her crippling devastation. She gets her to her feet, and they walk wearily together up through the streets of the village while staying wary of the fires. Geertrudia wallows to the point of retching. Victoria can barely catch her breath between crying and coughing as the cold night air dries out her throat.

They reach Victoria's house, where a cart was left out front. It was used to gather red mammoth beets earlier in the day and it was surely abandoned to join the efforts to search for the girls. Once inside,

Geertrudia stands at the window keeping watch for the monster, anticipating its approach. The lightning storms glimmer passes over the village, preceding the vivid details of Rode Heuvels return to darkness. The fires are spreading, and their light shines a dim shimmer in through the windows.

At that moment, the sound of heavy raindrops hammering from the roof reaches her ears. Victoria is at her desk, where she retrieves her red leather journal. She opens it to see the glowing vial beaming with light. It is alive with activity. She closes up the journal once again. When she turns around, she can see Geertrudia at the window. Geertrudia's tears glitter like starlight as they fall. Her eyes, wide, riddled with fear as they appear to be clawing their way out of the sockets. Surrounded by lurid orange and bruised red, she is entangled in the fire's slow approach, with its colors caressing the edge of her features. The light is animated with raindrops distorting the window. From the dark side of the room, Victoria wants to call her name. But she is paralyzed in watching her.

Raising her hand, she goes to speak, but neither air nor words come up. Taking a breath, she tries again, but she cannot conceive a thought. There are no words of comfort. There is nothing. The words are gone. Victoria can only be silent while enduring the empathy she has. She knows how it feels to lose the love of your life. She knows how it feels to lose a child. But their experiences will never compare, no matter how close in similarity they are. Even harsher is the reality that Victoria certainly couldn't know how it feels to lose her whole world in one night. For all her academic knowledge and all her skills, she sees her impact on the world reflected in Geertrudia's life. What can she do? For now she has nothing. She has no new knowledge to dispense. No words that could sow the wounds. Nothing to offer to kill the pain. "What can I do for my sister? " she asks herself. Sorrow tremors over her heart, knowing there will be no reminders of Jacop and the girls. How will she remember them except with the horror she is left with? With the options that are left, Victoria weighs that there will be nothing but to flee this night. Everything must be left behind. Geertrudia must leave everything behind. Victoria sheds tears for her. Powerless to watch Geertrudia's life be torn from her. Forced out of her home, robbed of her girls, and made to watch her husband be killed in front of her.

She is deeply empathetic, and still she is unable to find any path to be beside her and comfort her. What can she do when she is to blame for all her loss? There is no telling how far down this hole is, but Victoria wants more than anything to regain some resemblance to Geertrudia's life. How irrational she knows it is. There is no natural science that could resurrect her hopes, whims, and wishes. It is impossible. This is not a world of magic in which it can be whisked back to the way it was before today. The only way to make sense of the world is when reason can be defined. Reason brings about truths, and the truth is unmistakable. Victoria sees Geertrudia in the ruins of herself, and none of her is recognizable. Seeing the death of joy in a woman who was made of it is gutting. The night brings an approaching tiredness that she embodies. The woman standing there now is a different person, weary yet composed of assertiveness and fear, which serve as the fuel for her caution. She can't even help her understand how to recover today, tomorrow, or any other day. For when it was of her own experience, Victoria was younger. She still had a life to return to. She still had comforts and wealth to aid in her healing. She and her family didn't deserve this. Geertrudia survives now as a mother without children and a wife without a husband. Where does home exist after this?

The rain dwindles the fires to smoldering embers. The colossal presence of night returns, draping the village in giant darkness. With an unnerving anxiousness, Geertrudia begins shaking and tapping her palms against the wall as she whispers to Victoria in fear and despair, "It comes... Victoria, it comes."

It comes. Deliberate calamity. It stalks through the street with a mindset reminiscent of a chase. Its luminescence glows blue in the pelting rain, which carries dread that sets off alarms within Geertrudia. It will never give way to surprise, for its light leaves little to the unknown. It commits atrocities that are clear as day, without ducking into the shadows and unimpeded by humanity. The downpour's veil has put out the flames that covered it. The fire has burned away its black murky hair, the sleeves of its long fisherman's coat, and the pant legs at the shins.

Victoria rushes to pull her away from the window, stopping to see what she sees. As she gazes out the window, she internally remarks to herself, "That haunting glow. I have created an Adonis. Beautiful and monstrous, never succumbing to a mere mortal's ailments such as illness or fatigue. I have seen the death and perfection of mankind, and I have unwittingly unleashed it into the world."

With a grip on Geertrudia's sleeve, Victoria pulls her back. Hiding them both in the shadows against the wall. Just then they hear Laurens and Albertus from outside. Albertus can be heard yelling, but his words are indistinguishable. Soon there is a loud scraping across the ground. For a brief moment, all that can be heard are rain droplets, echoing.

Then suddenly all silence is broken. Crashing noise erupts. The cart from in front of the house explodes through the wall. Shattering wood screams. Fierce, unmitigated devastation happens rapidly. Victoria and Geertrudia are thrown to the floor and buried in debris. The sound of countless collisions of wood is deafening. Splintering beams and broken bricks disperse. Unsuppressed clatter of rain intrudes. The small space condenses more. The warmth of the house escapes, with the unforgiving weather taking over.

The wreckage quickly fixes. Stagnation lingers. Then Victoria's arm emerges. She uncovers her head. As soon as she is able to open her eyes and lift her head, she sees the figure of a man cutting through the rainfall in flight.

It is Albertus. He soars horizontally. He cascades through the air like a chicken that has been flung. Feet first, his body hits the floor. Tumbling across the red mammoth beets, shards of wood, and wet. He plunges into the wall. Quickly he comes to his hands and knees, drunkenly searching the debris. His movement was wild, like a cat chasing shadows. Finally his search ends, and he rises with both his hands narrowing tightly around the handle of an axe.

The cart lies on its side in the middle of Victoria's house. Albertus beside it readies his stance for a fight. A disquieting incandescence draws near. A cold pale glow enters the gaping hole in the wall, and everything in destruction's wake reflects it. As Victoria backs away in fear, she can hear the shudders of fright coming from Geertrudia. For her, the sight of the creature as it sets foot in the house reminds her of the hopelessness she felt the first time she laid eyes on Napoleon's invented De la Police. Uncertainty of her safety gripped her soul when she was in the clutches of their malicious regime. But this was a greater evil. For when in the clutches of this monster's dread, she knew what it wanted. She has seen its intention within its actions, and there is but one goal. To scorch the earth.

Victoria looks her over, and she sees a shard of wood has pierced Geertrudia's abdomen. She scrapes away the rubble and, with a hands-over-knife calm, slips Geertrudia's fingers into hers and hauls. Outside the torn wall, Laurens' head appears. A flushed, startled young man in a hole of obliterated timber. From Victoria's perspective, she can see him clearly; from his perspective, the house appears as a pit of consuming darkness. This is especially true as he is distracted by the monster.

Albertus rips a word from his chest, raw and urgent. "Run! Find the others. For God's sake, get aaway! The command shatters the air. Laurens hesitates as if the words have weight, then ducks and bolts, feet pounding in retreat. Victoria tugs harder, but Geertrudia's cry rips out. It's a high, ragged sound reverberating off the walls. Victoria turns, every nerve alive. The sound reveals them in their shroud of darkness. Steel-bright attention slices through the gloom. The creature lifts its head as if answering a summons.

They stand, like predator and prey, in the hush between breaths. Fifteen feet. Fifteen feet of cold, tight space, where time feels slow, yet her heart beats like quaking earth. No sound but the thinning of blood in Victoria's ears. The moment narrows to that distance, and in that distance she waits for her juggernaut to deliver dread.

Their eyes lock. Her inquisitive brain spins cognitive thoughts of her collective knowledge to assess the situation. No mind like a Frankenstein's as she thinks with a heightened velocity. Though only a second or two passes, it is enough as she mentally documents theories. Its hair has burned away, leaving nothing to obscure its eyes. Inside, they are protected from the rain, and there is little obstacle but the pressing constraint of time to analyze the monster.

Victoria recalls reading her mother's records of the witch trials , wherein ne entry she wrote of a man who was a prominent skeptic of allegations of witchcraft. An English physician named William Harvey. He reached his death at the age of 79 in 1657, but in his lifetime he was publicly recognized for a report that led to the subsequent pardoning of four women who stood trial for witchcraft. That was in a time when a death sentence was guaranteed for women who were accused. He would go on to write the book: "*An Anatomical Dissertation Upon the Movement of the Heart and Blood in Animals*." In it, he writes about recognizing the flow of blood rapidly traveling around the human body and diagramming a single system of arteries and veins. That map of the human circulatory system is evident as it radiates under the monster's glassy skin. Within the diversity of its venation and the burning flare of its eyes, she recognizes the light is generating from countless tiny flashes that hold its fairly uniform luminescence.

A repetitious glint of lightning is hauntingly quiet, but while Victoria's creature is seen in the company of lightning, those billions of tiny flashes explode with burning flares. She thinks how the ghostly glow coursing through its body could be bacteria trapped in a constant decay and regeneration effect. In another recollection, it was during her travels to the Americas that she recorded one specific evening. An evening where darkness reigned and her ship was cutting through light in the water. She would later come to understand that the algae in the ocean's far recesses created light in defense of feeling threatened.

"Is the electricity provoking the disease?" Victoria asks herself.

There is no time to ponder more as the axe Albertus wields ravages the creature's neck while it's turned away. Albertus jerks at the axe, intentionally tearing as much flesh as he can. The gore is abstract; bioluminescent blood sprays the air and paints the floor. Its flesh tears with a momentary blood loss only to close back up in healing with the blood dripping like white lava made of gleaming opaline, where every part that is beyond its light is contrasted in darkness. With the axe retrieved, Albertus swings again but with the intention to dismember the creature's arm.

The skin breaks. More blood is drawn. Albertus is shaken with disbelief when the axe bounces like a blacksmith's hammer against an anvil off of the creature's arm.

Victoria recognizes this. She remarks to herself that its muscle fibers have a density of metal. To fall victim to a precise strike from the monster would mean instant death. Thunder plays on like nature making endeavors to warn all life that they walk among the unkillable. Still, Albertus is not convinced that the monster is beyond defeat. Committed, he continues to engage in a death-defying battle.

From behind Victoria, she hears Bernardo. "Victoria!" He yells with a strained voice from the soaking rain. He goes to her, climbing inside the house.

"Victoria," he says again. He drops to his knees to wrap his arms around her. He pulls back, placing her face in his palms. "Victoria, are you hurt?" Victoria can see anguish in him. His apprehension for her welfare stirs her heart. Still her concern lies in her selflessness, and she replies, "It is Geertrudia. She is hurt. We need to save her." They both lift her and carry her out of the house. Bernardo can see at a glance the red leather of Victoria's journal. He leaves them both momentarily to grab it.

Then, escaping onto the street, Victoria looks back one last time. The monster presses forward in nonstop momentum, using all parts of itself as a potential weapon of bludgeoning. Albertus is outmatched as he becomes overwhelmed. He takes a devastating hit, and his forearm becomes broken, folding over itself like a deep rubber boot. The proof of its monstrous nature can be seen in its firm decisions to inflict harm. Without remorse. Without hesitation. Average men falter under equally physically demanding conditions. The monster instead propels forward with an endless battery. Like a battery, they are both made of energy, both unpredictable, and both dangerous.

The monster pounds Albertus' collarbone, forming a hump in his back. With certainty, parts of his bones have turned to dust. Before Albertus can collapse from the fatal blow, the creature grabs him by his head. He swings Albertus around, making him horizontal. In a vicious undertaking, the monster repeatedly belts the limp body of Albertus against the walls of the house. Thrashing him at the floor and against the cart until the man was mostly broken bones. A once tall and handsome German man who was ideal in his strength and health has been reduced to a tenderized slab of veal.

She contemplates, "My monster is the monster of monsters, for it is the sleepless and relentless erasing of good men." Victoria weeps in both remorse and terror. The darkness is a kindness because it conceals the vivid mutilation inflicted by her monster, while the light reveals enough to comprehend Albertus' lamentable misfortune.

Chapter 11

The Maker

A newborn baby. Her soft features radiate. Her fragile eyes are shut, resting heavily with a baby bonnet encircling her face. Her tiny fingers, flushed and warm, curled into her palms. The new mother, Ambroos, lies in bed while she lovingly swaddles her daughter. With her husband, Gerbin, peacefully unconscious in bed beside her, and her home without a single candle's flame, she absorbs the intimacy of her sleeping world. Bathing in the ambiance of rainfall and the occasional strobes of lightning that walk past her window from time to time. She is impulsive when the urge hits her to kiss her baby's head. Ambroos doesn't wish to disturb the stillness in the room and elevates efforts in her small movements to peck her baby on the head quietly and slowly. She lingers over her baby afterwards to sniff the purity of her scent. This scent is distinctly different from the odor Gerbin produces after working all day in the fields or returning home from days of hunting. It is not like the odor of her clothes when they have been sullied with the prying of salty sweat, nor is it like the smell of clothes that have dried from being washed. There are many scents in the world, endless in delicious aroma and equally endless in putrid foulness. No, there is no greater a sensation than that of the essence that can be detected in the scent of innocence. Impossible to replicate. Devoid of toil. It is absent in their domain, the whittled years of exhaustion carrying dreary unhappiness to the end of their day. No salt of the earth weighs on them. The notion is unfeasible to ever be drenched in the ocean of a broken heart. Being new to the world means not knowing about those pains. Ambroos knows there is no other smell like it in the world. It is purity.

"How long now?" she wonders. "How long before she can begin to feed herself? How long until she is able to crawl away from me?

How much longer will my baby remain a baby, and when will she speak her first words, marking the beginning of when she no longer needs me? Irrational, she knows. What a quizzical concept. There is a possibility that she could never be in such a quandary, for since she can remember, she was close with her mother, even up to her last days. There are truly worse happenstances, like those of her sister Geertrudia. She coils at the maddening thought. If her daughter was unable to be found, there is no force of nature that could keep her from doing whatever it takes to find her. Her husband is able-bodied now, but she knows he has not seen what enablement she can be capable of. In previous years, Gerbin had once fallen ill due to consuming poisonous berries. She aided him back to health for weeks. Nurturing him as he vomited. Feeding him when he couldn't eat. Cleaning his bowel movements from his sheets. She was adamant about her consistent care, even sleeping at his bedside most nights. He knows that her efforts are the reason for his health returning. He knows she would rather wither to a stalk of wheat before letting him die. She loves like she is growing an orchard with prolific trees. She is unwavering in her attendance, never allowing their strength to fade. She gardens with a labor of love and then patiently sees in time what beauty flourishes. How she admires Geertrudia and Jacop's union. With such an example to look up to, she mustn't be far off from loving in a way that keeps it strong and healthy, she hopes.

There is a sound of trudging feet and heavy heaving that joins the clatter of rainfall. The front door swings open. It cracks as it meets the wall. The sound of wind and rain overwhelms the room. Gerbin wakes and frantically leaves the bed in a terrible wildness. Quickly lighting a lantern. Victoria enters their home first, leading the way with Geertrudia's arm draped over hers and Bernardo's neck. Once inside, Gerbin shuts the door and bombards them with questions. His confused anger turns to worry and concern when he realizes the weight of the matter as he sees Geertrudia's wound. They laid Geertrudia in the bed. She is soaked from the rain, and her bleeding quickly changes the color of the white sheets. Ambroos gets up from the bed while cradling her daughter to pacify her from waking. Ambroos is launched into a grievous state.

"Geertrudia!" She wallows involuntarily, "What happened to her?" raising the question to Victoria. "What befell my sister?!" Gerbin goes to his wife to soothe and comfort her. Bernardo tells them about the monster in the village, ending with a confused, "I don't know where it came from. I had never seen anything like it before in my life, except..." He stops and turns to Victoria. "...except ... for that glow."

Victoria is sitting on the bed with Geertrudia. They are staring into each other's eyes, with Victoria's filled with remorse and shame and Geertrudia's burning with resentment. Their hands locked together.

She knows Geertrudia wants her to confess to them what the monster is. "What? What is it?" Ambroos presses. Geertrudia asks her in a faint, bloody voice, "Why did you do it? Why did you make it?"

"Why did I do it?" Victoria remarks. She ponders all the while sniffling and catching her breath. Shedding unwanted tears, she replies, "So that... so that I may have a child again. So I may be a mother again."

"What do you mean?" Ambroos inquires, "I don't understand."

Bernardo responds to Ambroos, saying, "My god, she made that monster. In the streets, it is destroying the town. It just killed Albertus. It is a giant. Made of both the darkness and rivers of light."

"Victoria?" Ambroos poses for her to explain sharply, "Do Bernardo's words ring true? Have you conceived such a child?"

Victoria stands up to face Bernardo, Ambroos, and Gerbin. "Tis true. Be forewarned, the imagination may find no tether in my explaining that, in the stead of a natural womb, my monster found its rearing in the cold destruction of my natural science laboratory. Eight years ago, I fled in fear for the same reasons that compel me to flee tonight. By account of my eyes of the past and the present, I know of this monster to be the first of its kind, in that it is the ever-progressing flow of carnage that is unable to be reasoned with. It is unkillable; with each wave, it will only heal, regardless of even the deadliest blow. Still it persists, for it hath long forgotten its connection to humanity. I am afraid to face such a monster. I am afraid... of a monster that murders... with a terrible inability to reason."

Victoria explains the demise of Susanna, Madelief, and all others who have perished up to this point.

All the while, the rain halts, despite the electrical storm still bustling with activity. Regardless of the downpour, it was not enough to put out the fires. Thudding steps in the quiet streets of the village. The monster's beacon-like presence can be seen from afar as it makes a destination that leads out of town. People are watching it in the darkness of the fields. Staying low to the ground, three pairs of eyes survey cautiously from afar as the monster flattens a path toward the windmill.

Augusto whispers, "Let us move." Yvonne and Zoe shoot up from the ground. Together with haste they nimbly take flight. Their noses are numb. Their breath is heavy. Despite the mud that has gotten into their shoes, they make their way back to the village hurriedly in spite of the ruthless autumn elements.

Back inside Gerbin and Ambroos's home, Gerbin is frustrated and proclaims, "Surely it can be killed." Victoria replies to him, "Its lifespan can't be measured, nor have I known death to come to those who share the same disease. There was one man I studied who had been alive for as long as 5000 years. There was no fatal wound he could not recover from."

All in the room are floored, and momentary silence chokes them. Gerbin stomps his foot forward, "How? In what world are such things possible?"

Ambroos steps in front of her husband, still cradling their child. Her capturing look puts him at pause. It is a look that beckons him to be of some understanding. "Love, it is our world, where all things can be made possible." Ambroos says to Gerbin. She continues, "I hath laid splayed open upon a bed where Victoria reared our child to the light of life. My thoughts were of goodbyes. I was confident in the coming of my death, for there be none such return from feeling the autumn's stony draft kiss my innards." Gerbin's eyes swell up. Ambroos continues, "She staved off death for me. Now, my love, have you ever known that to be possible? Yet, I am here. An impossible... possibility." With tears beginning to shoot down his cheeks, he pulls Ambroos close, kissing her head repeatedly.

"Despite my words," Ambroos says, turning back to Victoria, "Tis quite a feat. I myself am struggling to comprehend how it is feasible. Be there some explanation?"

Victoria starts to tear the top layer of her dress into ribbons while she says, "I concocted a mix of blood, each cursed with the same disease. What resulted was an abominable change in the main constituent's genetic characteristics. Though theoretical, I hypothesize that these mutations are hereditary. In some cases, the mutations were also recessive. Victoria can see she has frustrated the men, but Ambroos has a set conviction to follow along, and she says, "Elaborate the meaning of recessive."

As she responds, Victoria continues to wrap the ribbons of fabric around Geertrudia's wound. "This means that a reaction occurs only when there are two copies of a disease, while in some cases the disease remains dormant, and in others, a single strand of the disease can be sufficient to trigger a reaction." To achieve my hypothesis, I was lucky enough, in my lifetime, to encounter a handful of generations that are carriers. This is how I was able to explore the underlying mechanics of their physiology and, most importantly, their disease. They all share closely similar traits." Victoria is interrupted by Bernardo, "There is no time for this flapping."

Gerbin asserts, "We should listen to Bernardo. Be it, if we are in danger, we mustn't squander time to act. Now, surely it has a weakness."

Victoria ponders briefly, "Possibly. I fell witness to it being stopped momentarily when it was hit around its neck." Victoria briefly turns to make eye contact with Bernardo, noticing that he seems to be formulating ideas. Victoria continues speaking, "But getting close enough would mean certain death. That is how Jacop and Albertus met their fate."

"What of fire?" Gerbin exclaims, "Nothing survives fire. If this be made our weapon, we could outnumber it. Surely, that could work, yes?" Gerbin presents his idea, putting his hunting mindset to work. Victoria considers his ideas before responding, "Fire does slow it down. We saw it buried in a mountain of flames. Still, it only allowed us but a few short minutes to elude it. Please, we must make haste. "Gather a few items of food to carry," she says, but before she can finish, the sound of the front door opening interrupts her. Augusto, Yvonne, and Zoe step inside.

"Children," Gerbin says, relieved. Yvonne comes forward, "We have taken all the children to the school. Along with what elders would come."

Victoria smiles at Yvonne, "You brilliant child."

Yvonne continues, "It was I, Zoe, and Augusto who heeded your cries. Our mothers trusted your warning as well. They stayed behind to gather food and blankets, should we need to seek refuge."

Zoe says, "We returned to help Gerbin and Ambroos get to the school." Yvonne then asks, "What do we do now?"

Bernardo answers quickly, speaking over top of Victoria's answer as he says, "We fight!" And she says, "We go west." Victoria gets up from Geertrudia's side again. "No... we go west. There is a town half a day's travel away. We will meet our doom if we remain."

Augusto speaks up to confirm, "The monster. It presses onward toward the windmill. We saw the monster just moments ago while crossing the fields. Let us take our leave before its return."

Victoria is the only one of the adults who acknowledges Augusto, and she is the only one to respond to him, "Brilliant child, you are most correct. Let us take our leave. Shortly after I have gathered supplies, I will be joining the rest of you."

Bernardo aggressively inserts himself in front of Victoria. "This is your doing! You should remain here and see its end! Obey me; you shall not flee." Victoria may feel some fear, but it is not as strong as the obedience shown by dogs to commands. Though she feels angered, she is of a calm, stone-skinned demeanor.

"Fear not, I will stay here with you. I will fight beside you." Bernardo claims this as if it offers some reassurance.

"There is no glory to be found here—" Victoria struggles to speak as Bernardo grabs her by the shoulders and shakes her in a fit of hysterical rage.

Bernardo yells in her face, "You will stay! You will kill the monster!" She punches him to the ground. It doesn't end there for her as she stands over him, repeatedly punching Bernardo, maneuvering around his safeguarding hands. She stops when he starts to cry. In between his whimpering, he says, "On my mother's love... on my mother's love... I have to do everything I can. This is my... my home. My only home. I must defend it."

"Then you are a fool, and you will perish at the monster's hands." Victoria proclaims as she moves away from standing over him.

Bernardo continues, "By my God, I live in Rode Heuvels. My home is Rode Heuvels. I will die for Rode Heuvels. Revenge for Susanna and Madelief. For Benji! That is foolish? I care not then; they deserve retribution." Bernardo says. Gerbin retrieves clothes, and while putting on trousers, he says, "I will stay and fight."

Ambroos drops her head and steps over to Geertrudia. Victoria argues with Gerbin, "You mustn't!"

Gerbin rebuts, "It was not long ago she was with child! She is unable to make such a voyage." He explains, gesturing to Ambroos. They continue to argue, and Ambroos kneels down near her sister. Now crying, she presses her head against Geertrudia's, listening to her struggle to breathe.

She holds her baby up. "Geertrudia... her name is Geertrudia. We chose it today." Ambroos tells her older sister. She looks at her sister to see a faint smile as she learns her niece's name. Ambroos realizes she will soon lose her. She presses their foreheads together. "I love you. There is a paradise in knowing sisterhood. I... I love you." Ambroos soon contemplates that her husband will meet a similar fate. That notion is as devastating to her as the sky falling. She contemplates that it is a shame because if Gerbin does not return, their daughter will have to grow up never knowing either of her parents. "For I will be a hollowed-out woman, and not even the ghost of me will come to rise. We will walk, and with one hand I will hold her hand, and the other will be resting on his gravestone. How will my beloved rest in death if I am crying over his grave forever?"

Bernardo has since gotten up from the floor and continued in the conversation with Victoria and Gerbin. Victoria sees on his face he is crafting some kind of plan. He asks her in a quiet voice up close, "What if I drink the vial? The twin?"

"Then you risk dying." Victoria whispers back.

"Would it allow me the same strength?"

"There is no telling what it would do to you. You will not take it."

Ambroos walks up, but her vision is narrowed to only Gerbin. She tells him, "I have lost my brothers, my nieces. Soon to be my sister. We will flee our home in refuge. I... will not... forfeit you. I will not submit all of my given love for a foolish gallant act. I will not allow you to die." She tells him, "What joy will come in watching our daughter grow up if it is only accompanied by the sadness of your absence? Food will be flavorless. You said that to me, remember? I will fall deaf to the beauty of music without you. How dare you not suspect that I love you at the same or just as much. I never knew you to be a cruel man. But if you fight, and you perish, you will be void of a kind legacy, as you will perform the cruelest act upon me. "You will take my heart with you to the grave." She sobs. Gerbin hangs his head in defeat to sob with her, pulling her and their child close.

"Vi...Victoria... Vi...Vi...Victoria." Geertrudia, almost indistinguishable, calls out for Victoria. The room turns to Victoria, and they all idle to watch her go to Geertrudia's bedside. The air is thick with turmoil that is now anticipated to worsen. With the oil lamp resting against the wall, the room is dimly lit by a flame's orange light that stretches itself to reach the dark corners with bouncing shadows. Ambroos can not contain herself and collapses into weeping. Victoria kneels down beside the bed, and all in the room move in closer. Victoria gently holds Geertrudia's hand. With her chest weak and her face warm from concealing the dam of tears, Victoria asks, "Yes, Geertrudia? What is it?"

"Moge God u vervloeken. Moge God u vervloeken." She mutters, which is Dutch for "May God damn you." She says it again, faint, soft even, but still the clearest she has said it: "Moge God, you vervloeken." Immediately after the spoken word, she quickly inhales and spits a mouthful of blood in Victoria's face. The room groans in dismayed surprise. When Victoria has wiped her eyes and is able to look up again,

Geertrudia is unmoving, slumped slightly with her eyes lazily hanging open. Ambroos wails as the quiet of the room reinforces the passing of her sister.

Victoria tears into herself within her thoughts, "It is I. I am the wretched maker. It is the cruelty of my negligence. I have allowed my ego to sink to the depths of the ocean so that this woman can express her resentment and have her final say. I have no hate to give. I feel only lament, regret, and shame for having made myself worthy of recompense.

With a thud and rushing feet, the front door swings open. Victoria gets up to investigate. Her journal lies on the floor sprawled open, face down. She drops to her knees, flipping over her journal. The vial... the twin, it is gone. Gerbin announces, "It is Bernardo. He has left us."

Victoria quakes and utters under her breath, "Bernardo... no."

Chapter 12

At The Grave Of Dreams

Wilhelmina steps outside her house just as Bernardo runs through the village. He screams frantically, "Everyone! Grab your lanterns! Grab your torches! The monster runs for the windmill!" Jacintha and Tessa step out of their homes as well to see Bernardo, and he continues, "As one, we must burn it down!" Let us take revenge! Let us burn the monster!" Bernardo continues to the stables. Victoria is running. Chasing after Bernardo. She arrives in time to see him fire from the stables on horseback. He is holding a lit oil lamp and riding in the direction of the windmill. Before she can reach the stables, another horse runs out, galloping into the open fields. Once inside she finds there are no more horses. She continues running. She goes after him, trying to scream to get his attention, but the cold is stealing her voice. Her muscles burn in exhaustion. Bernardo stops his horse a short distance from the windmill. He hears Victoria in the distance. "Stop! Refrain from this, Bernardo! Please!"

She sees that dismal glow of the vial in Bernardo's hand. "No!" She screams mid-sprint. He pulls the cork on the glass vial, and its ultraviolet glow disappears behind Bernardo's lips. Having drunk the vial, she stops. Her jaw ajar, unsure of what to do now. She can't stop whatever is about to happen.

"What did you do?" She utters wearily.

Bernardo rides up to the windmill. He dismounts, with his horse tame enough to idle without him. Only a moment is spent assessing if his horse will run off. As he turns around, the eight-foot monster has stepped out of the windmill and stands before Bernardo. He looks upon it afflicted with fear while staring at the fireflies that flow through its veins.

It grabs the horse with both hands, trapping Bernardo in the middle. In the commotion he lets go of the oil lamp. It drops at his feet. Breaking. His legs catch fire. The flames spread quickly, engulfing mostly his clothes. While fighting the flames, he breaks free from the space between the monster and the horse. For a short time he runs blazing as a human pyre.

Victoria is catatonic as she watches helplessly. Her heart steps outside her body. She bears witness to the monster's astonishing physical power as it grips the horse by its neck. In a single turnaround it is able to lift the horse off its feet and disturbingly swing it horizontally. To Bernardo's misfortune, he is in the way of its course. With a bludgeoning blow, the horse's hide clobbers him. The thrashing hurls him thirty feet or so closer to Victoria. Breaking through her paralysis, in the depths of despair, she runs to him with shattered breath and the weight of a thousand sorrows anchoring her down. Each step a battle against the void. She collapses toward him, her weary soul reaching out to him, surrendering to relentless anguish. Both overwrought and brittle, she crumbles as the resilience left in her burns out. She pays no mind to the mob of villagers running behind her. Their oil lamps and torches emerge on the windmill like a herd of flaming birds soaring through the field.

Bernardo is a screaming bonfire as he lies burning to death. Victoria weeps while watching on her knees. Palms up and powerless. She cries to him, "Bernardo! Bernardo!" She weeps under his screams. To her, his screams challenge the thunder that bellows. Never has a sound cut away at her skin the way his screaming does in this moment.

Then, his arms and legs stretch three times their length. At the mortifying sight, Bernardo begins to kick and flail, making Victoria cower backwards. She watches as his body changes inside of the flames. She can see morphing happen as his face grows with bone marrow. A snout extends out, tearing the skin on his face. Within it there are teeth on top of teeth that sprout in rows of sharp daggers, pushing out the normal teeth all at once. Then a phthalo green spreads in the form of elaborate scales, like snakeskin. Taking on a dragon-like appearance. Soon Bernardo's body starts to bulge as every muscle in his anatomy is growing. The muscles grow four times their normal size, pulsing with vascularity. The muscle growth leads to bloating, causing Bernardo's entire body to become bulbous and grotesque. With each change, Bernardo reacts. He feels everything. The excruciating pain of his bones growing and his skin stretching... and tearing... and burning. The fire changes color, lashing the flames in a deep vermilion red as a chemical-like aura distorts the smoke's plume. Countless large blisters start to rise before bursting with black ichor. Each pop sloshes and splashes when it explodes. Skin and muscle become untethered to the bone, falling away piece by piece. The agony of his screams draws gradually toward an end. His bones crackle as they turn to cinders.

After watching the horror of Bernardo's demise, Victoria is defeated. Her nose scorched in the scent of his torched body that carries the aroma of rusted iron and rotten potatoes. Sobbing, she trembles in the cold. She is only kept warm by the fire that burns on Bernardo's bones. The language of fire is all she can hear as it rustles.

Darting past her is the mob of villagers as they descend on the windmill. The monster has disappeared inside, and the horse lies dead nearby. When they reach its foundation, they begin to set the windmill ablaze. They use their torches and smash their lanterns against it.

Victoria considers walking over to the windmill and burning alive inside. She ponders to herself, "I see no reason why I should not be in there as well. It is I who should be burned at the stake. Oh, Mother, I am sorry. I know you would shun such speech, but I speak so foul, having given the world nothing but a creature of desecration. Father... I am sorry. You wanted not but goodness from me, but it is with a weary heart to which I propose that the goodness will die with children and has died with what life you made of goodness. There is no goodness my guilty soul can claim now."

In the flames, the monster emerges once again. Its silhouette rippling with heat and its emanation piercing the inferno. Making a victory in its defiance of death. Calling attention to its firm will and pure force, it returns outside. Making a mockery of such a dangerous element as fire by passing through it unimpressed. With the villagers huddled together, they gape at the monster's mountainous bulk. They stare in disbelief at its veins, aglow like molten white rivers. They watch in horrified awe as the monster, impervious to pain or mortality, emerges triumphant from the firestorm.

Above, the sky convulsed in blackened wrath. Bolts of lightning tore through the clouds and fell, not to earth, but to that towering colossus. Jagged strikes seemingly feed perverse vitality into its luminous veins. With every crackling surge, the creature's glow flares brighter. Thunderous winds shriek in protest. Lightning bombards the windmill. Victoria can see now that the electricity is in fact causing a reaction in which the monster's illumination brightens. The brighter its veins glow, it seems the more violent and uncontrollable the monster becomes. She knew what was to come next was her monster's onslaught.

In a blitz of lightning bolts, the monster insanely attacks. It goes from one villager to the next in a rampage. There is no escape from its vicious wrath. The creature drops its fist down on a woman's head, which does not impede its inertia. Deflating any boning. The creature's knuckles cut through the air, colliding with a man holding a torch. The assault is so calamitous that the right side of his torso is obliterated, removing his pec, shoulder, and arm all at once. The man falls, dropping on his torch and setting him on fire. Chaos explodes in flashes of raining lightning. The creature reaches out with gnarled hands, lifting a man by his ribs that soon burst like hollow gourds, continuing to squeeze through him until the man falls in half.

Shock seizes Victoria. Her hands shake involuntarily. She could decide to get up and run away if she wanted, but instead... she stays. As rooted to the earth as an elder tree. Willing herself not to move from this spot and be the recorder of testimony. Documenting the horrors. Viewing the bane of gore as it massacres the people of Rode Heuvels. She holds herself responsible and therefore will not allow the benefit of looking away from the slaughter.

Villagers run to elude the brutality of its clutches, and in a ferocious tirade, it tramples them. Dismantles them. Squashing bodies beneath its feet. Flattening some. Folding people in on themselves. Crushing them into nothingness. The monster kills with a speed of eradication that steals even their screams. The witnessing of a tyrant stomping out the existence of those it deems valueless.

For Victoria, her thoughts have always been ever-voicing. But for a few moments, Victoria's endless inner monologue has fallen silent. She craved this quiet to memorize every tremor of terror, every loss. A self-punishment by bearing witness to the horror. In her self-imposed penance, she vows not to blink, to not look away, so that the world might someday know the true shape of this atrocity.

Before long, her thoughts articulate themselves again. "I have ridden through the sandstorms of Egypt. Crossed the ocean to the Americas. Lived in luxuries that sound as profound as dreams to commoners. I have loved, I have seen love, and I have been loved. Plentiful have been my trials and tribulations. Many harrowing battles. Some as a fighter and some of wit. Now, I anchor in the carnage storm. Clear here that inside my life I have felt never such a ruination, in all my experience, in all days on all my battlefields. Being chased by death had the presence of fear. There was a version of me, a scared me, that visited through time. Never like this. Such powerlessness. Unforeseeable hopelessness. To witness what I hath never seen before. At the undesirable destination, here lie the graves of my dreams. All that was once flourishing is now put under, to be the soil of flowers. Time will watch them be abandoned and overrun with the dried up death of greenery. I sigh with sickness in my heart as I look at it. Look at it. My juggernaut. It kills, decimates entirely, without so much as an ounce of anger or joy. Labor of love cannot define it either. It stalks, thrashes, and bustles mindlessly. Blood covers its glassy skin. Perhaps it is the disease. Perhaps it is a natural force that is running its course. Acting involuntarily, and yet, that this could be a possibility... does not change that I am in hate with it. Resentful... regretful. I wish I never gave birth to the destroyer of the world. I relinquish my welcoming heart for it. For the forever of night's darkness, for the forever of daylight's burn, until time steals the remembering of the names of the trees and the air of the world depletes and all life that has ever been known is choked out. The pain of wanting you, foul monster, gone, goes on for a forever, and it is in that means of forever that I will be in hate with you. My child. My monster, my creation. Perhaps... it is more. Is there some inconceivable connection it has to nature? Truly a key to titanhood. Does it command the storm itself? Does it lay waste with purpose? Is there some goal it is unable to communicate? Or, quite possibly, is someone in there? Imprisoned. Tortuously transformed. Incapable of control? I wish I could know, truly. Still, I relinquish my love because of it. For in truth I hold some semblance of pride. It disgusts me. My creation is strong, without contest. It is alive. Alive in a way an inquisitor would define. Alive... it's alive. Moving forward with momentum exceeding expectations. It's remarkable that the anticipated limitations of motor functions, strength, or speed never manifest themselves. How amazing. What a tremendous achievement. How fucking revolting. I decline with no anodynes. Fall away from things enamored. I refute pretensions of pride, therefore, and any that of joy as well. I will be haunted for the precedence of my days with the sight of the emergence of that celestial fire that burns in its veins from under its lucent skin and the hot white pits of its eyes."

The windmill's fire is like a giant, dancing in the storm. Victoria grips the grass and soil while swaying because her body is drunk with exhaustion. Her nerves are stinging spider bites. Her eyes are wrung out of tears, and her throat is ripping dry. She would stand and walk to death now if only the ground would stop spinning back and forth.

"No. There is no blame better placed than upon one's head. I did this. These people gave me a life again, and I took theirs away. As I watch the monster tear through them, I wish for bolts of lightning to strike me down and punish me. There is no world coming that changes for the better. No world I could possibly create. Henceforth, as I look upon a maker of death, how foolish, cruel, and stupid I am to have ever envisaged a destiny where one is to be idolized as an angel. I am ill within... that within myself... there was ever a foolish conception... to dream."

• • • •

1816, THE ARCTIC.

Victoria stops journaling to acknowledge that her fire has been out for some time. The will to keep it going has evaded her. It may be a seal on her fate if she does not keep the fire burning. Then again, she knows that. With hurt on her heart from recollecting the past, she continues to journal. Damning herself on purpose.

She writes, "As I rested upon the dirt, with my hands I gripped the earth with panic as a drunken disorientation took over me. I felt nauseated, and a dizzying spin disrupted my body. It was a sensation of gravity giving way. It was then I had finally given up. These weren't deaths. These were my neighbors, my friends, and the flame of their lives was snuffed out in an evening. My neighbors, my friends. I still wish I had the strength then to get up. I wanted so terribly to give mine own self unto it, my monster. To let it do what I had feared most. To deny me my story and any legacy I could hope to have. I ran from death not simply in fear of a painful demise, but in truth I feared most to be erased. I lived with a hunger to obtain an extraordinary life. How awfully foolish of me to have squandered the last eleven years depriving myself of all its beauties. I remember nights of painting in the winter and the candlelight reflecting off the windows. Nights we danced in the ballroom when we could dance until we fell asleep listening to the band play their cellos. But mostly sitting in spring at the edge of my garden, enjoying the heart of my life in the warm smell of flowers as they bathed in the sun. I feared all this to be erased. I never allowed myself to forget the horror under the shroud of night's maw, where I forfeited what was left of my dreams. It was then I heard a quiet voice say, "Miss Victoria," as they grabbed my arm and helped me to my feet. It was Knelis. He had survived with only a broken arm. He found me and rushed me away while there was still time to spare our lives. I did stop one last time to look back. Now arrayed in red, the grass and water all reflected the red of the windmill varnished in fire. The blood in the field glistened. And in that blood-soaked night, the juggernaut remained, standing victorious in the fiery scene surrounded by death. Its wretchedness to never be brought to justice."

Chapter 13

The Year Without A Summer

Urgently, the quill darts out, word after word, across each line, like a messenger running out of time. Victoria writes, "I traveled with knelis to the city of Knokke. He had frequented Knokke with Jacop to do trades and knew where to find a place for us to sleep. Shortly after arriving, we caught up with Ambroos, Gerbin, and the children. Ambroos had a discussion with the kids and Gerbin; she fabricated a story and stated that there was no monster. That it was a traveling troop of the De La police on their course back to France, and she spoke fictitiously about them burning down the village and casting us into refuge. Ambroos spoke with conviction that this was the story they would tell from now on and that there would be no mention of me. A couple of days after our arrival, we were in the local market. In the midst of the crowds of traders, salesmen, and patrons, there was a moment when I saw it. Hiding in a shroud. At least it seemed that way until traders began to converse with it. Maybe I wanted to see it again. Vexed with its presence imbued in my eyes, the scare was enough to send me running. I knew then that I must go, for I have seen how lives are destroyed by the death that follows me. That night, I deliberately left without a word to anyone. I kept moving with this sense that I was being pursued. I'm certain I caught a glimpse of it again and again in every town I stopped in. I left the Kingdom of the Netherlands to discover that the world was changing, as a once unstoppable Napoleonic army had now completely retreated to France. Regardless, I was quick in my dealings to avoid the violence of Napoleon's contrived De La police while traveling south through France. Finally, when I was in Italy, I boarded a fishing vessel disguised as a man. I worked on the vessel until we arrived in the Arctic, where the ship momentarily became enmeshed in the ice. Eventually, when the crew freed it from the ice, I disembarked before the ship could depart back to Italy. I stranded myself in the Arctic tundra as part of a plan to lure my creature despite that there being no way of knowing if my creature still follows me. It is a position poised in paranoia. This running has persisted for three years. I am finally without rations. With the amount of time I have spent in rumination along the way, I made a decision to trick my creature into following me to a place of no return. If my paranoia is eventually validated, then I will have lured it away from the world, unable to harm another living soul, trapping it in the Arctic. Other thoughts had crossed my mind in my ruminations, such as what I was truly afraid of. I revisited the thought that I was afraid to be erased and examined if that is what I truly feared. Even that of death was a simple enough answer that long sufficed for the question until I recognized within myself, over time, that what I truly am afraid of is that I will never have a page in history. I fear becoming just another nameless, faceless woman forgotten in the black spot of history. What I am most afraid of is dying insignificant. In my pursuit, I hath sealed myself to this very fate. Throughout my lifetime of research and academia, I have sunk lower than the feared insignificance, and I possess less than what could be considered infamy. I have erased myself. I have become titleless; therefore, I have become nothing. A valiant toil to gain the title I deserve. It was in the late hours where I paced in retrospect, that I stumbled upon this epiphany to give up protecting myself for a dream I will never see. It was time to take action and do what is necessary to stop the unstoppable. To put an end to my creature's treachery and quell my fears of a dismal future. A future where it will surpass us all. Whereas, a destructive being made by humans, unable to better mankind in our search for advancing natural sciences, efficient medicine, and human progress, will ironically come to eradicate the need for people. Beautiful, diverse, creative, loving, dreaming, wondrous people. Now I am here. Trapped in the furthest reaches of the Arctic with no hope to escape alive. This is the best chance I have to do the right thing. Now I must give up these thoughts, as my ink will soon come to freeze. I will close my last log remembering him. My greatest love. My final hope as my life fades into the colossal embrace of winter's breast is that I can gather the strength to see in my memory his eyes for the last time. Those brilliant eyes, the heart of my life. I have spent all my years obsessing over my dreams of creating a medicine for him, some form of aid, or even a cure. I have followed one prospective clue to the next, traveling all over to find answers for him. I suppose I could not ask to change the past, for there is no telling if I would be endowed with more time with you. Given how easily history has unfolded and how fickle life can be, I could just as readily could of been condemned to less time with the gift of him. There are people living the whole of their lives in happiness. It does not matter whether one lives a quiet, simple life or a life in high society. There is truly a possibility of their unhindered happiness. I have regrettably let the pockets in which the years of happiness resided escape me. The years in which happiness was at its most powerful. My life with you was short-lived; no will can make that time obtainable again. Happiness lives within small chambers of life. I now understand that everything was merely a series of obstacles leading to the discovery of these chambers. I invite every life to learn appreciation for those small chambers, for it is always with devastation that all of existence comes to reclaim them. The most powerful happiness I have ever felt was the happiness I shared with him. His kindness was a life force, of which whimsical stories have been written about to be unattainable. Therefore, how astonishing it was to receive you freely. The way he looked for me in all spaces. The way my name, spoken by he, felt deeply supernatural. I would never know a greater absolute love. It was all for him, my darling F—"

Impulsively she gasps, staring at the written page with all the stillness of a ship frozen in ice. The ink has frozen. Victoria tries to scratch the rest of the name, but she quivers, and her attempt is weak.

Never to finish the name. She looks over the captain's quarters, acknowledging that it is a dark 300-year-old icebox. The cold has long set in as she closes the journal. Victoria thinks that, of all the ways the earth takes life back by swallowing it in its nature, a tomb of ice is the one she would be most amenable to. Between the battle of drowning in water, the vicious submission to fire, and the gruesome disorientation of poison, freezing is where death makes you a bed and coos you to rest, for sleep is where you'll find peace. The cold is a blanket that never gets warm, and the colder you get, the more you abide by the dose of sleep. Not realizing how weak she's become, she attempts to stand up when both her legs give out and she falls to the floor, knocking her journal down with her.

Victoria finds she is overexerted, as her efforts are great to get up, but she is unable to see success. "To what need," she thinks to herself, "Welcome this with dignity. My duress is pitiful; why pile on more shame? I resign in this way, not without shame. If my father could be in this room... if he could see me, I know I would feel ashamed. If he were to be in this room... he would... he would... he would pick me up. He would tell me there is nothing to be ashamed of. I can hear his voice still -

Bear the brunt of the world's bold brass as all the world must; do it with integrity and do it without fear, 'tis doth there be no condoned shame if neither were in possession, for the world's brass cometh unimpeded. It shall come for us all. If 'tis so, then thou art without the will to fight, then I seest no shame in a soul that is afraid. There is no shame in death. I seest woe, and I seest hate, but there, in no soul of any woman or man who walks with goodness and still denounces to those in dying to be shameful. Be not concerned with the words nor notions of those who ne'er gardened within their self, a bed of goodness to prosper. Nurture your goodness. Your trees, flowers, food, and all substance of you, in your will, are the goodness for others, for there is more the world holds. My Victoria, you have but brilliant

power in every trickle of time to give the world more good. For there is more than only the harsh brass of the world.

My father embodied kindness and goodness like a morning spent in the shade of trees. A reliever of harshness, he made it easy to be around him. He was an effortless man to love. He would sooner see himself die than allow for anyone to be in his stead. He was only ever pressing about a few ideologies. That death follows Frankensteins, that life was made for living, and from that which I can recall most, that the proliferation of goodness is always worthy. You could deem someone worthy by their goodness. You could deem any fight worthy if it saw the preservation of goodness. You could deem self-sacrifice worthy as a means of protecting goodness. You could deem love worthy if only goodness is what flourished. My father, how I hath wronged you. I have been careless with your legacy, giving way for it to be carried off like a voice on a draft. Yet still, despite my horrid pain in lament, I know there is no act I could be expected to perform in which you would not cloak me in your pride. I still remember when he told me that he has seen imperfection with his eyes as much as he has breathed air. However, he has only ever understood perfection as something invisible, a concept played with in imagination and dressed in metaphors that illustrate how a collection of imperfect things can appear together. Never imposing perfection on me. Even at the heights of my childhood, when I saw other girls be punished for going against what was expected of them, my father encouraged me to do everything. He wanted me to obtain all the trappings of an educated man. He encouraged me to strive to be more than that, even. To be a woman of erudition. That the sole purpose of my life was to be defined by me. Not to serve a husband and bear his children. The influence my mother had on my father was so impeccably vigorous that he implemented her ideologies daily, from my upbringing of never lacking in education to a household order founded in reason. I never saw him in a moment to make a decision in which he was separated from himself. A great amount of his essential nature was rooted in the beliefs of kindness and goodness built with ironclad fervor for his positivity that no ideology could combat. No matter the presence of wretchedness and foulness in an army of words, they would be met with no opposing infantry but instead an unassailable structure commanding acquiescence. Therefore, when it was apparent he was conducting himself in what could be my mother's wishes and when time called for it, the whole of his self had to be put aside, and he did so happily, without ego, without strife. My father never remarried after my mother's passing, nor have I ever known of him taking on another lover or mistress. My father and I traveled together quite often, and on one of our journeys to the inherited ancestral Frankenstein castle, I recall him explaining how my mother fondly missed the motherly nature of Germany. She spoke of it often, of wanting to return there all the years their love bloomed, and he had promised one day he would take her, and she could feel the warmth of Germany's bosom again. It brought him great lament to keep his word not once while she was still alive. He chose the words engraved on her headstone plaque that resided under the feet of a statue chiseled in her likeness, where her naked body is draped in a thin fabric while she cups a lotus flower before her face. The words engraved read:

"The whole of her life was spent weaving her love into others.

'Tis, in truth, still so much of her here."

It was possibly his way of keeping her memory alive by instilling her values in me so that I could then share those same values with the world. Unbeknownst to me until later in life, 'twas his application of love for my mother that I would adopt. I would never disown the memory of a love, and in my conviction have seen no reason why I shall not preserve each of their legacies. All except... my fathers, I suppose. My father, my gentle, beautiful father. The nights we would read together by candlelight. Oh, Father... I still feel the warmth of the room with you near. You, in your chair while I was nestled in the window nook. Some nights by oil lamp and a many by the flicker of candlelight. Sometimes until I fell asleep against the glass. Happiness felt so quiet and impervious back then. If only I could hear you reassure me again now. If only."

She starts to pay close attention to her heart. She feels a slowness. A delay. Her pulse creeps to a pause frequently, but she pushes for it to speed up breathing with struggle. Shortly, there is a long pause in her heartbeat that jolts her awake when it picks back up. She momentarily opens her eyes with a hazy screen over her vision. She realizes she has spent hours with her heartbeat in observation. Her eyes ease closed once again. Her coat and gear visibly frosted over. It is with positivism that Victoria is on the brink of freezing to death.

The sensation of a hand running under her head compels her to attend to consciousness. She can tell it is an immense hand in the way it pillows her head in size, or so it feels. She opens her eyes to a slit. What she sees kneeling down before her in a red hooded shroud is her creature. A lonely tear falls out with no resources left to drop much else. Strange. There is no pain. She remembers the violent thrashing of the creature glowing with radiance. There is no glow. There is no thrashing. Absent is the expected grip of its crushing palms. This creature is considerate in that its hands and movement are gentle. With her vision blurred, she tries to fix her sight and open her eyes more.

The creature removes its hood. That black stringy hair has grown back except where the stitches reside on its scalp, in the middle and across, and it drapes the creature's pale, almost translucent face. She can't see clearly, but she knows it perceives her with a curiosity. While propping her head off the floor, she hears it say in a deep, resonant, Scottish accent, "Mother."

Chapter 14

The House Of Strays

A low-hanging tree branch showering in midday sunlight along with the rest of the green growth in this springtime meadow is hovering tranquilly at rest. The yellows of minuscule flowers that grow in the grass make the greens look lighter. The vibrancy of all the colors creates a blissful haze. A young child rushes through the area, swatting a low-hanging branch with his hand. Their breathing is heavy, pausing for swallows to keep their throat from drying out. It is a young boy, and he keeps moving forward, seemingly in search of a new route to take while passing up dead ends. The tweed overalls he wears come halfway up his shins. His black leather shoes are small, close to the size of a six year old's. Cutting through a puddle, the child ignores it to continue running for his life. With his mouth agape and his cheeks and brow under his light brown hair cooking pink as a dog's paw, it is evident this endeavor has been going on for quite some time. The outright imperativeness of his nerve-racking disposition paints the implication of a dire situation.

He comes to a stop, pushing down the body of loose shrubbery. He unveils a pair of gigantic, leather, cobbled shoes. He lifts his head to see that the monster is in those shoes.

It is standing upright, dressed in dark-merlot-red wool clothes. The child is diminished to nothing more than meager in comparison to the monster's colossal form. Shadows form upside-down triangles under its eyes. A dark place in the meadow hidden away from the sun. Under dimness. Its semi-transparent skin has a gloomy, grey, deceased shade. The blue of its prominent veins is scarcely hidden. The creature has black somber hair, a matte coat resembling a wolf's fur, bloodless marshy yellow eyes, and ivory teeth that appear brighter against its thin black lips. Running would be futile; they are done for.

"I found you!" With his tiny voice, the boy yells. With his tiny voice the boy laughs. His laugh is so tremendous that it is filled with all the might of his tiny stomach. The boy's stomach is pushed to its absolute limit, resulting in a mighty-tiny laugh. Playfully he accosts the creature, who then falls back into the shrubbery as it is clearly rendered powerless to the young boy's attack. The boy tugs at the creature's shirt, throttles its wrists, and restrains it from getting up. Surrendering to every manipulation, the boy directs it to move, for he was just too powerful. The boy laughs continuously as he conquers the monster. Doomed, there was no way they could win against the likes of the mighty-tiny boy.

Later that day, the creature sits in a rocking chair in the dusk that descends on the German wilderness, gripping a book while the boy sleeps in their lap. The boy is tuckered out from an afternoon of terrorizing the creature in the meadows. Behind the rocking chair is a clothesline where a petite woman in a white dress wrapped in a blue apron who has burnished red hair hangs clothes to dry.

That evening, the creature sits at a dinner table still gripping the same book. A window rests at its back as it sits on a bench built into the wall. Docile, it eats slowly and with refined social behavior, unlike the two children at the table. He sits across from the woman who is feeding a young girl who looks to be four. In a Scottish accent, the boy asks the red-haired woman while he holds a snarl on his nose and without any peculiarities of anger, "Will you feed me as well?"

Without losing their place in the book, the creature spears a potato on their plate and raises the fork to the boy's mouth. With a mighty laugh, the boy chomps the potato off the fork. The woman looks upon them, indulging in contemplation of her evident happiness.

Shortly after dinner has concluded, the tapping of a dog's nails on the wood-boarded floors can be heard in high performance from the lounge room across from the dining room. The young boy riles up his giant Leonberger dog.

The dog has a thick coat of fur with a lion-like mane of a charcoal color. The rest of their body is reddish-brown. The dog's beady bright yellow eyes follow the bouncy boy. His trotting makes his fur bounce, delighting the four-year-old girl as professed in her giggling. The book the creature has been reading is closed now, resting on the bench beside them. The red-headed woman, still sitting at the table, talks to the creature with zeal, using her hands to animate her overzealous expressions at times.

It is the spring of 1810 in the Southeast of Germany, and the following morning, as dawn's light cuts across the alder and pine forest canopy, the creature sits outside near the front door. The creature sits outside without a book, simply clasping their hands together while watching the sunrise. As the creature looks on, a thought crosses their mind, but it remains unexpressed because they appear lifeless in their stillness. A gloomy, expressionless face forever adorns them. The metal clanks on the door latch as it opens. With her red hair parted down the middle and loosely falling to her mid-back, the woman of the house steps outside and takes a seat. Her skin is of a pale complexion, and her chin comes to a point. She adjusts her arisaid dress, lifting the green skirt off the ground and wrapping it around her legs and then covering up her shoulders with a red and white tartan. The two look at each other; she smiles her high smile, peering back at the creature with her deep-set eyes. The creature stares back with its droopy, downturned eyes, and it says to her, "This morning has gifted me with my memory."

With a spring, the woman sits upright in her chair, eagerly awaiting for them to continue.

• • • •

"Fire. Thunder. Destruction." The creature speaks of the night it was created in 1805. It opens its eyes to blistering white flames that charred the floors and walls black. The rain, invading through a collapsed ceiling, could not quench the fire's power.

"I was born into a laboratory amidst a disaster." Shortly after waking, they remember the feeling of an uncontrollable rage running through their body. They remember being scared by the thunder's roar and the blinding flash of lightning. This extreme anger was involuntary and felt like it was dictated by a force of nature. They explored beyond the laboratory to a high balcony. There, it was confronted by people. People that it would never recognize. People it relentlessly killed.

"I remember the lightning dispersing like the dance of two lovers coming to an end."

The creature says in their deep, coarse Scottish accent, "I remember, for that is when I stopped being afraid."

The creature stumbles through the burning castle and eventually makes their way downstairs. Nearing the front entrance, they stop to look at a large painting hanging in a room. "The painting is of a woman. There was a plaque on the bottom. It read, "Victoria." The rest had been scorched black."

"If I was born of fire, in that castle, and she was the master of that castle. Then that shall be the basis for my imaginative assumption that there is no other who can claim to be my giver of life. Until I can know more, Victoria is my mother."

The creature steps through the front doors, their clothes reduced to ashes. They wander across the bridge and pause to look back, witnessing the castle engulfed in flames. Continuing down a winding road toward the arch entrance of Mill Valley, they cry out into the rain.

"I then pleaded for help, for I felt remorse. The heart I sensed in my chest yearned in repentance. I grieved as I recalled the atrocities I had committed moments before, and I sorrowfully sought help. I didn't know what was happening to me. I had no control when I killed those people. I could hardly speak when I was as eager as I had been to understand. I felt as if I was newly born. A child's mind, naked, alone, and scared."

A crowd begins to grow. The townspeople gawk and sneer with disgust. Some shudder. They form a mob, screaming with intent to run the creature off, all while toting mindless religious chants like immoral extremists. The overwhelmed creature eludes the vile mob as it disappears in the forest treeline outside of town.

"I never returned. I need not cause another uproar among those people. I recall their fear. They were as alone and as afraid as me. As I recall it, they were not children; however, their actions conveyed they were, in their minds, children still. Aged by time in wrinkled shells with no merit of wisdom withheld."

One morning, the creature finds themself wandering in a frost covered wilderness, "Fragile. The frost breaking in my step. Crumbling away at a touch. The grass, flowers, and leaves without control yielded in submission to a force of nature that froze them. I beheld then that it is I who share their equal burden, to be an organism in life that must endure what nature dictates. I saw then that I was delicate. Equating my pain to that of flowers suffering in winter. I perceive now it was then that I had only the one comparison to reflect my woe upon. Be that as it may, what was true then holds true now. Taking it upon myself to make a nature in and of myself of the same nature as the flowers. What quiet peace the flower must timelessly be acclaiming in nature's inescapable silent serenade. I wish not to be in the realm of red handed death. The maker of fear. I want a stillness. I wish to be the flower admiring the meadows. Lost are my wishes on the listening ears of nature, I am sure. I know now it is only a season away that I must helplessly watch a beautiful thing suffer as the flower freezes over again, against its will."

Over the course of the winter of 1805 into 1806, the creature traveled from the Southwest of Germany to the Southeast, living in the woods the entire way. One morning, late in January, while the red-haired woman was chopping wood near her wooden cabin, she saw the eight-foot naked creature walking through the forest. Frightened, she takes her axe with her to confront it. Yelling, with her axe raised, the creature cowers, and she restrains herself to recognize this unfortunate creature abandoned in the snow.

While it feared getting a rise out of her, she put down the axe and welcomed the creature to come with her. It was a slow process, but she did everything she could to foster a calm atmosphere. Once she could get them inside, she helped clean them and clothe them. Over the next four years, she taught them to speak and read. The creature quickly excelled in both. She was gentle, patient, and understanding. Despite eventually being able to communicate, they were having trouble recollecting who they were and where they had come from, forgetting so much of the traumatic killings at their hands and the town that ran them off. It was a year after their arrival that, in a lesson of reading, the creature heard the name of a character in a book of Hesiod's "Theogony."

"I like... this name. I choose to this... for-for-for to my name." The red-haired woman nods in approval and says, "Prometheus? Very well, we have found you a name. A beautiful name for a beautiful person. Prometheus."

The red-haired woman likes to sit with Prometheus after breakfast has concluded and see if there is more that they remember. Even when they reach a stalemate, she continues to find out how far Prometheus's progress has come. She lingers with them after dinner as well. This is almost an unspoken tradition that stands up week after week and then continues over the years. On one occasion Prometheus asks her, "Catriona? How did you get here? How did you and your children come to be living in the forest?"

Usually enthusiastic to talk, Catriona pauses for a moment to look at her children, who are in the other room. "I was a girl in Scotland when I was traveling with my family. I am not sure how they died, but I awoke to find both my father and mother had passed. I wandered until I found the nearest village, where a widow took me in. She showed me kindness. She said she gave me the love that was meant for the children she ne'er had. I came of age, and a traveler came into the village and stole my heart. I married him soon after and traveled with him. We traveled for years together, and I was never exhausted by his company; 'twas mine own many cups of joy. William was his name. He was Germanic, and the time came when we sought travel to return to his land. On our journey, we were passing through Germany when we discovered two abandoned children." She points to the children in the other room. "I named them both. The oldest is William, after my husband, and Adelaid, named after the widower who took me in as a child. William seemed two; Adelaid was under a year at least. My husband, William, knew the fondness of my heart as I laid eyes on abandoned children and saw the child of myself. I thought of all the futures that would be destroyed, and I wanted to give my effort to care for them, for I knew that for these children, being abandoned will surely destroy their world. He would not bear to have me lament. Therefore, we took them in as our own. Soon, we arrived in his land and settled into our new home; it was not long after our arrival that William fell ill. He peacefully passed in the night. Six months did pass, when on a winter day, you arrived in the snow. Sickly looking, naked. You appeared hurt. The world had abandoned you. I could not simply disregard you so easily."

In the years to pass, Prometheus would recall glimpses of a memory, and they would try to recollect the rest, but it has been without success. Till now.

....

CATRIONA AND PROMETHEUS bask in the morning sun that has climbed to suspend over the forest during their conversation in 1810. Prometheus concludes, "I find it most prudent to prepare myself for my imminent departure. You have no reason to feel secure in my presence, as I have become acutely aware of the egregious nature of my past deeds. It would be unwise for me to impose upon you the burden of my history. I resolve to seek the fair lady depicted in the painting, though an age has passed, and the path back to the castle has slipped from my memory. One truth remains clear to me. I see myself as the monster that the townsfolk proclaimed when they cast me into the wilderness. As a monster."

She shakes her head in disagreement. "I have seen what is positive of your nature. I have examined you carefully in many possible actions. I accept without doubt that goodness is true of you. It is evident as many times as my hand is wet when I pull it from the river. I shall prove it; what is your favorite color?" She asks. Prometheus says, "Red, I have grown an affinity for the sight of your hair."

She blushes and continues, "Well... What is your favorite food to eat?"

They respond, "Your gingerbread in winter."

"There are no makings of a bad person within you. No deficiency of a positive moral nature. You possess qualities in a remarkable degree that never find a place in the hearts of men elsewhere. You are no monster. Even the sight of you is beautiful. You will be staying. You will feel the warmth of light all your days, and your belly will be full. You are wanted. I want you here."

"This is a happy life, here."

"This life together is perfect." She says. Prometheus decides to abide by Catriona's wishes, and they do not leave.

When autumn came, dry copper-colored leaves piled around the cabin, and their fragrance perfumed the icy air.

The winter of 1810 abruptly arrived, and the cold was callous, burdening Catriona's health and the health of William. The illness forced them to be bedridden most of the season. Prometheus took on Adelaid's care along with all the housework. Prometheus fed Catriona hot meals and soup to help her regain her strength. Some days she seemed to get better, only to fall back into crippling sickness the next day. William recovered before Catriona and was always eager to assist Prometheus whenever needed. With winter soon coming to an end, Catriona awoke one morning having finally beaten her illness. The light of her softness bloomed once more throughout the house. Nights of conversations after dinner continued, and games of chase and tickles with the children periodically occurred in the warmth before the fireplace on endlessly white days. The laughter of William and Adelaid defined the moments; they obtained memories of joy, and that joy added a key ingredient to the fortitude of those walls where happiness forever lived untouchable.

In spring, Catriona exclaimed at Prometheus, "Come with me!" She took them by the hand out into the first spring rains. "Can you feel that? That is what beauty feels like."

"I can." Prometheus says, "Each drop plays a chord in me as though I were a piano. Nature makes music that can ne'er be heard, only recited for the soul to feel."

Catriona stops moving to stare at Prometheus in the heavy downpour, trying as much as she can to look at him. "A soul. The beautiful song of rain for a beautiful soul." She lays her arm from her elbow to her fingertips against Prometheus's chest. She pulls at their shirt with no force, as a gesture to lean down. Prometheus leans down. Catriona slowly presses her lips into theirs. She pulls away to take a close look at Prometheus. "Can you feel me?" Catriona asks with ardent eyes as she struggles to see through the rain, waiting for them to contemplate.

Hours pass long after they returned inside and dried in front of the fireplace. They both reside in brown leather chairs.

Prometheus says to her, "Your beauty is of a strong nature. In earnest and in truth, one's self is void of sexual desire. There is a love I am capable of, though I am not sure what days may need to pass before I conceive an affection to give you in return. To speak of what is materialized, there is no lover's passion I can compose; therefore, I am not a being that has set an endeavor to mate, nor do I have any desire to find one. I may not possess a way to portray it, but I must profess my wonder, for life is within its infancy. There is a winter that I wish to see on the abyssal waters of the ocean. Rain on the vast desert. The life of spring in lands that see only snow. There is much to discover about myself. So much I must learn of myself if I am ever to find the woman in the painting. Victoria. I am trying to discover the sweetness of life I can obtain despite the bitterness it has to offer me. I feel sensation and not pain. Those are answers that she surely holds. Therefore, in order to find her, I must leave this place.

Catriona was wounded. To love and not be loved in return is a monster no matter how it is gained. A town lies to the east, just an hour and a half away on horseback, where she happened to run into a fisherman from whom she has purchased twice before. In their conversation he tells her that he will be traveling to work in Bruges, in the Dutch Republic, to fish in the North Sea.

In her return home she tells Prometheus, "I spoke with the fisherman today. He is traveling up Germany soon to fish in the North Sea. I asked him if he needed a second working hand. I professed I knew of someone who wants to travel." With her eyes wet, she looks at Prometheus from across the dining room. "Do you want to leave? Would that make you happy?"

In a decent timely manner he responds, "I would most assuredly prefer such a notion." Softly said, withdrawing enthusiasm for Catriona's pain is all too obvious.

The next week Catriona, William, and Adelaid took Prometheus to town, where they were seeing them off. Before he would load into the fisherman's carriage, Prometheus lingered. William cried, and it made Catriona struggle to fight back her tears. William asks, "When will you be back?"

Catriona answers William, "They are not coming back."

Shocked, William exclaims in his mighty-tiny voice, "You must come back! You must come back! I will miss you terribly! I love you, Father." Catriona breaks, weeping into William as she picks him up. It is the first time he has ever proclaimed Prometheus as his father. Catriona feels the gentle touch of Prometheus's immense hand persuading her to turn. She looks up at them. They lean down and say, "I shall return someday. Dear Catriona, I love you." They slowly lean in. Catriona is without hesitation and collides with them to kiss their lips with verve.

"Here I have a name. A family. Here is where I will find the perfect life of a quiet flower. I will come back to you." Prometheus tells her.

"You will?" she says through tears. "I will." She hears them say. Soon the three of them watch as Prometheus is carried away by the carriage, growing smaller and smaller until they disappear into the hills.

• • • •

THE DANGEROUS NORTH Seas, October 1813. Wave after angry wave punches the fishing trawler. White mist explodes up against the ship relentlessly. The rough waves toss the small vessel around as if with a ruthless vendetta. Both the fisherman and Prometheus are in the wheelhouse when lightning suddenly pulses through the purple ocean sky, illuminating it in a blink.

Inside the wheelhouse, Prometheus says, terrified, "No!"

"What?" The fisherman asks, "What is it? Art thou afraid of a wee bit of lightning?" The fisherman screams in an equally serious and hoarse voice while he fights to steer at the helm. He soon loses his grounding in logic from what he sees. Bewildered, he watches Prometheus hold out their hands as their veins bloom with an ultra-violet blue light with a milky white color at its center. The light rises as it permeates through their veins. All the while flashes of lightning and the acoustic shocks of thunder are echoing during the creature's transformation into rage.

"Lightning... Lightning bad." Prometheus musters words as embers spark along the contours of their face, each glow resembling a twisted branch. Their eyes burn, casting a sickly, otherworldly light that beckons foreboding. Amidst this spectacle, his features become a cruel parody of a living man, as Prometheus's zombie-like mask of rage overcomes him. A clash begins as Prometheus slashes with an elemental wrath at the hapless fisherman. All the screams are drowned out by the ship's creaking timber, the auditory onslaught of every thunderclap, and the tactile sting of wind and searing water. The boat begins to give way to the roaring ocean waves of the deadly North Sea. Here, in the embrace of chaos, the trawler's bones groan in protest as they succumb to the relentless, pounding heartbeat of the storm. Waves monstrously dance, their uproarious passion echoing the wrath of some vengeful sea god. The ship's fortitude begins to buckle under nature's fury. The assault of decaying hope and brine, and the surreal, almost intangible power of the North Sea, swallows the boat into a spiraling oblivion.

The Zwin North Sea Coast, November 1813. Ten days later. Meshed with sand and the wooden debris of the fishing trawler, Prometheus lies on the shore. Moved only by the pulse of the tide. As they stand up, they are grieving, for they remember everything about the brutal killing of the fisherman. They weep, which renders them unmotivated to leave the shores as they feel remorse for their guilty conscience. Prometheus, the tragic titan, caught in the cruel, majestic machinations of nature.

It is still dark just before the sun is to rise, and Prometheus, still wearing his fisherman attire, walks offshore into the Zwin forest. As they traverse the forest, they reach the treeline and spot a nearby windmill. Before reaching the windmill, Prometheus notices two little girls heading in their direction. Afraid, they turn back to the forest to hide within its canopy. They come to a pond. They pass by its still waters and find shrubbery to conceal themselves. They are a hundred or so feet from the pond. They lay in the grass in leisure. Most of the hours are spent in fear that the next storm will come, when they will again be rendered futile by the forces of nature. How Prometheus wishes they could understand the occurrence more and why it happens. Maybe then they could piece together a way to counteract it. For to watch in protest of it all and still feel so worthless in the wake of an absolute superpower digs out a cavern in the heart. There is powerlessness in looking upon the helpless as they are slaughtered. Prometheus is highly cognitive and perceives the sorrow and pain of people with intelligent empathy. Prometheus philosophizes in their rumination that immorality is the state where intelligence is absent. How cognizant, comprehensive, reasonable, and intelligent can one truly be if one was never educated in the many understandings of empathy? They fear the lightning because, in its presence, Prometheus loses all intelligence and becomes merely a brute destructive force driven by temper. No empathy, humanity, or intelligence prevails.

Nightfall comes and goes, and as a new morning arrives before the sun can dawn on the day, Prometheus hears a scream. A grim, dim vision dulls the colors of the forest. The sky was grey with stirring phantom clouds.

A child's scream echoes again. There is some crying. Then there is the crying of a second child. Prometheus can see that a light frost decorates the trees and leaves. They must lie still to not draw attention to themselves. The sound of cries abruptly stops. There is something rustling in the leaves and the grass near the pond. Twigs can be heard snapping. The noise of grass being brushed over repeatedly. Slowly Prometheus sits up, attempting to make as little noise as possible. A dreary blue light is flowing through the air.

Peering through the shrubs that conceal them, they see an unpleasant man. It is Benji. He stands up from the pond's edge. His trousers around his calves. As he pulls them up, a taller man who is thin in stature comes up from off the ground. He turns around, and Prometheus can see he has half-lid eyes and a bushy mustache with grey peppered in his black hair. He is smiling as he pulls up his untied trousers to cover up his naked groin. Prometheus hears Benji say, "The village will be in strife when they find what you've done to these simple girls."

"And you will hang with me for your inexorable actions." He says, laughing. Benji says with a smile, "Maybe we are wrong, Bernardo. Perhaps they will award us for ridding the village of the burden of looking after the simpletons." Together a laugh erupts between Bernardo and Benji as they fix their trousers. Bernardo commands, "Come, together we will put their corpses in the pond and cover them in loose grass. All shall fail to manifest foul intents. They shall be none the wiser."

As Benji walks closer to the pond, he questions, "What of that incessant woman? Victoria?"

Bernardo replies, "Fret not, brother. Verily, I have shown myself to be a worthy distraction. Though she be learned, that bitch shall ne'er ascend to the heights of a man's wisdom."

Together, Bernardo and Benji toss two bodies in the pond like empty plates, discarded half haphazardly after dining. These men make little effort to shroud the bodies in loose branches and grass. At one point, they even kick dirt over the bodies as if trying to cover a minor mess rather than an atrocity.

Prometheus waits in silence for more than a half hour after the two men have long gone. When they were sure the men had gone far enough, Prometheus rose out of the shrubbery. Slowly they make their way to the pond. In the clearing's eerie silence, Prometheus can hear leaves crunching under every step. Blades of grass encased in frost snap. They feel their heart beat faster as they become more and more afraid of what they'll come to find. Their worrisome breath grows louder, adding to the few ominous echoes. When Prometheus sets their eyes on the pond, there are a few seconds of stillness within them. Anyone would need to take pause the way Prometheus does to understand what they were looking at. The scene is a combination of all of nature's materials, resembling a collage or even abstract art. The way one can look at an oil painting and then take the time to decipher the brushstrokes of each color. Like the mind unfolding the image until it becomes clear and an epiphany hits. Prometheus sees in the water, under the twigs and branches with loose grass and chrysanthemum flowers shrewdly skewed about, the sides of pale white faces. They barely float above the water. Motionless.

Without sparing another thought, Prometheus explodes into a flight of distress, plunging into the pond. Walls of water are thrown around as they tear through the pond to get to the children. Careful not to hurt them, Prometheus is still gentle to remove the shrubs that cover their bodies.

With a conscious courtesy, Prometheus puts each child in the fold of their elbow and carries the young girls' bodies out of the pond. They look at them and see how much they resemble the mighty-tiny William and Adelaid. Prometheus cannot refrain from weeping, stopping time and time again to sob. They shake them repeatedly, the smallness of their bodies feeling all too familiar. "Wake up. You are safe now. I hath got you... you... you, you are not abandoned. Be mighty, children;

do not fret. You are... safe." Prometheus can't control the sorrow that distorts their face while weeping. "You are safe... now." They cry to the trees, to the uprooted chrysanthemums, and to the settling waters of the pond, for there is no life in the girls to hear Prometheus's harrowing cries.

The sun moves up, but a greyness keeps the day from harnessing a warmth. Prometheus never lets them go. Lamenting over a thousand futures lost. Mourning the worlds destroyed. Prometheus never leaves them, even as dusk occurs. They sit with their legs folded for hours, often swaying them in a cradle. A cradle Prometheus wants, more than anything, for them to feel, instead of whatever their last pain may have been. Prometheus never leaves them, even as darkness settles on their eyes. They remain there with the girls. Never abandoning them. Holding their bodies... until a storm comes.

Dim orange light resonates from the oil lamps behind Prometheus. They lay the two girls down to rest on the shore of the pond. They see the lightning flashing through the forest canopy in the distance. Prometheus is in such a state of remorse that it has become an agony. They recognize Benji's voice when he calls him "monster." Turning around, Prometheus knows it is out of their control what will come as that burning bright light travels through their body and they say, "Monster." They hear gangs of thunder crashing in tens, ferociously attacking the night before blacking out.

When they come to consciousness, the early sun has risen, and there are the makings of a windmill burned down around them. Smoke still searing from the embers. Exploring the fields, they find bodies burned and dismembered. It is a horror, and they soon remember that all of this was their doing. Prometheus understands this and takes some time to grieve in regret. Prometheus thinks to themselves, "One who is intelligent is empathetic, and one who is empathetic feels remorse. I can't change what I have done; therefore, the goodwill within can still be ethical and do right by the ones I have wronged." Prometheus gathers every last one of the bodies and digs them individual graves. They use planks to mark where the graves lie without anything engraved on them. Except for Susanna and Madelief, whom he buried close together side by side with the engraving on their plank:

"*Here lie two mighty girls.*"

Prometheus soon travels west, and while in the town of Knokke, in the crowd, they catch only a glimpse of Victoria. The face of the woman in the painting that is imprinted on their mind. Her visage resides in thoughts and dreams that defy explanation. Mother or not, there is no one else with the key to who they are or how they were born. Prometheus never stops in pursuit of finding her. Even as she leaves the Kingdom of Holland and descends down the border of France, he tracks her, always being one step behind, all the way to the heart of the Arctic.

Chapter 15

An Answer To Dreams

Her monster cradles her gently and, while holding her head, says, "Mother." Prometheus looks on her dying body with harmless curiosity.

She thinks as she feels her creation hold her by her shoulder with their other hand, "The torture that I must have a moment to prepare myself for the prime evil horrors to come is true justice for my crimes. It was impudent to even persist in the chase with the endurance of what I have known to be its impenetrable spirit."

Prometheus asks, "Are you Victoria? The master of the castle in Germany? I have come a long way to find you." Victoria can barely react, but she feels alarmed at being asked a question by her creation.

"I am," She replies with much struggle, "I am... she. Victoria. I was once the master of a house in the south of Germany. Is there...n-n-n... no malice? Y-y-you are here... to enact... revenge. Are you not?"

With a calm demeanor, they reply, "Any expectations of malicious intent are found solely within one's imagination and therefore are placed upon me without positiveness."

Victoria self-reflects in her thoughts, "Is this my creature? The blood-soaked titan from whence I saw what was like lightning glow within its blood and tremble in its hands? Where is my carried dread sentencing for the wretched human crime of meddling with the realm of creation between gods and man? Their voice alone is baffling, like music etched with raw emotion that brings my heart to tears as they speak refined and dignified with an elegant opinion. It is more. It is alive."

"Victoria," Prometheus says, "I have known you in my dreams; a face that I saw in the fires to which I was born. I have seen you in a thousand dreams gone unexplained. I have learned much about the world from the comfort of books, and I have compared you to the literature that has taught me. By those standards, you resemble what is to be my mother. Are you my creator? In all these terrains of the world's map, is there anything that holds me in connection to you?"

A tear falls from the corner of her eye as she fights to nod "Yes."

Prometheus is overcome with weeping joy and says, "I have wanted to know you for more than three thousand days. To be in your presence and learn what 'will' I was made with. I have long ago decided who I want to be. There is no longer a part of who I am that you can influence to reflect a part of yourself. Know, from whence I stand, that I wish for you to know of my good will, despite my abandonment by you. Know that I am not a long forgotten shred of what was once human. I am a forgotten person. I am loving. I am loved. I am compassionate. I am good. I am not a monster. Thus, I am also not without remorse and regret, as there is an illness within me that is dictated by the inescapable whims of nature. Powerless, there is no controlling it. You are my creator? Should I call you demon? For why else would a good soul abandon a child and leave them to die? Are you void of love? Furthermore, are you void of love for me? Be it that there may be no validity to these notions, propose it is a wrong thought, and you are merited to be dreamt of in an idol's form. Provide evidence that I was not made to be one's property but in truth a wanted child. Give me a name. Name me as one's own wanted, loved thing! It is what I deserve. For I am no creature nor monster. I am a person."

Victoria sees now that she has wasted so much time running from her regrets. Victoria Frankenstein sheds a tear, and after a struggle to muster words, she raises her hand, reaching to rest her palm upon her creation's cheek, but with her strength fading, she falls short. Her creation leans closer and rests their face in her palm for her to then brush their cheek with her thumb.

Lying on the floor beside Prometheus, she can see her journal. She must have knocked it off the desk when she fell.

She reaches for it. Prometheus deduces that she wants to pick it up, and they hand it to her. There is no thought and feeling that is without the knowledge that she will soon be met with her demise, and Victoria sees the ripples of her actions, the honor of her father's name, and her final opportunity to make amends for him and for the life of her creation. Victoria pushes her journal into their chest and says, "You... you are of the family name Frankenstein. You were wanted... in your creation. Your... n-n-name... is... Frankenstein. You were wanted. You are loved."

She remarks to herself within her thoughts, for her lips are too weak to speak, "I was wrong to allow my fears' dominance over my dreams. I have wasted my remaining years selfish and hardhearted, where I could have seen that small chamber of happiness once again. Now is no time to make a shallow artifice appear as a dilemma. In death all is without dilemma. Instead there is a parallel of joy and misery in knowing the success of reviving life that is evident in a healthy and promising child and being too late to know of it."

She wipes away the tears Prometheus sheds, for they are shaken with fulfillment. They find beauty in the good nature of their long-sought maker. Victoria says, "Find it. Within my journal... find the answers you seek. In my instruction you may... fall in love with mercy. Learn from me... how dangerous is the neglect of even one child."

Her eyes slightly roll back as she grows weaker, and she fights to keep consciousness. All her words become faint. With the energy she gathers, she says as clearly as she can while looking into their celestial eyes, "You are an impossible possibility. The universe is a raging rapid that overtakes us all. Yet... here you are. My brilliant child. The universe, stilling the waters of all its moving parts... for you... to be here."

It is with the last of all her strength she tells Prometheus ahead of fainting, "There are so many apologies you did not receive. Apologies, the child in you deserves, and apologies that, what you have become, are owed. I must leave you now, but not without what you are owed. I am sorry. My impossible child. I am sorry for my mistakes where you were made to bear misfortune. You will come to see the hardest thing to find in this world is kindness. Make more of it for those who need to see it exists, for themselves."

"Mother?" Prometheus says as Victoria closes her eyes. "Mother, why did you make me?"

But there is no answer. For a moment, she opens her eyes; the foggy sheen has left, and for the first time, she lays her sight upon her creation's eyes with clarity. Her evoked thoughts would be the answer if she could find the strength to speak.

Her voice echoes the walls of her mind, "Why were you made? I could not bear to go on in this life without seeing you again. Without seeing those perfect familiar eyes again. My brilliant child."

As she recloses her eyes, never to reopen them, she can feel her fears resign. The gentle cradle of her creation holding her head and body close in lament. The doses of sleep weigh heavy, and the cold slows what beating life she has left. Abandoning ambition and submitting her spirit's flame.

There is an echoless abyss where she conveys her last thoughts, speaking to herself. "My heart is exhausted. I feel my heart as its strength stops. I feel no pain, and I did not anticipate a painless departure. It is more like a sensation of being a child again. I am! I can see it! I am a child again. I can see it so vividly. I can feel it like it's happening. Reliving a moment I know to be true of my past, but I feel it consciously as though it is happening now. I am a child, falling asleep at the window nook of my childhood home in London. I can feel that heavy exhaustion steal my power and weigh down my eyelids. More than a familiar place, it is one and the same. It is just like an evening when I had dozed off against the window in the library. As I lay there drifting further into slumber, I feel the firm arms of my father as he carefully lifts me up. I know he means to carry me through the house to lay me down in my bed. As we pass through the hallways, I can smell the smoke of each candle he blows out. I hear the soles of his shoes tap the wood-boarded floors. The creak in each step as we ascend the stairs. I feel my head rest against his chest as I wrap my thin arms around his shoulders. As we enter my bedroom, I feel a pleasant draft coming from my open window. A grateful emotion gently blankets me, knowing that a loving, caring soul such as he is taking my tired burden off of me. Safely carrying me to a peaceful rest. I thank my father, but my words sound far away, barely to be heard. I thank him for everything he's done. He lowers me down with a cautionary handling as though I were a fragile egg. He overexerts himself to see that I am laid down softly. While I lay there suspended in a painless bed of comfort, I feel him still there caressing my hair for the last time. Before I drift off into that void of unconscious darkness, I hear the deepness of his kind voice softly say, "Dream now."

• • • •

PROMETHEUS HOLDS VICTORIA'S lifeless body. Cradling her close while brushing her hair back. In the frozen dead shell of the ship, the wind of the Arctic tundra seems too large as it whistles outside. Prometheus weeps for what wishes there can no longer be. The answers they still seek. The want that still resides within them. They cry, and that is the pain Prometheus can feel as they are subjected to the unrelenting whiteness of the room. There is a beating heart underneath their chest, and it yearns for wounds of its young self. Those moments alone from when they first opened their eyes and began to be alive echo throughout their being. They come upon a lonely age that leaves them feeling hollow. A spiritual fear.

The tremors in the ship's carcass get stronger with the rise of the winter storm. With time Prometheus ruminates in their lament, "There is a hollowness as barren as abandoned catacombs to wonder what small corners I may ever find again where love will welcome me. What kindness there may have been of her to bestow on what child she thought of me to be. A kindness of hers I can no longer know. Surely I must accept this as a punishment with integrity. What life is more deserving than that to be in the mud with the filth, cast out? I am no rabid dog, an animal, fighting to survive and acting as though I've never known the love of a mother. I am willing to be punished for my crimes. However, I feel a sense of timelessness within myself. No older do I feel, nor do I feel a decline of vitality. Somehow I know that time will wash over me, like the passing of rain, and I may remain paying for my atrocities in morality. Be it as though there are no urgencies, nor the treatment of time as though it were fickle and short. Therefore, I cannot allow myself to bear resemblance to the monster nature makes of me. There are no eyes that will set on me and see what lives of naturalness. Earthy be my flesh, and my touch as cold as clay. Grotesque and abnormal, to be the embodiment of all the world's fears. Victoria... what more kindness was there of you? What more kindness will I find?"

There is still so much more they wanted. They can feel that any hope of knowing the nurture their young selves need ceases altogether. It is like searching for a burning candle in the dark and finding it only at the end of its wick, experiencing the warm light of its glow for just a moment before its flame perished. The time and the effort to reconcile is positively an impossible eventuality. Those may be what the tears are for. Their pain is not from losing someone they hardly knew, but from knowing there will always be a part of themselves that now can never be whole. Years spent dreaming. Woe, for what dreams must end.

Acknowledgment

We, the authors, would like to thank Marco Rios and Laura Desantiago-Rios for all of your support over the years. We would have never been able to survive without you. Thank you for not abandoning us, and thank you for believing in our dreams.

Keith Long, for giving Victoria Frankenstein its first review and having so many kind words to say about our work. We appreciate you. Martha De Santiago & Julian De Santiago for being a lighthouse in uncertain times. Tim Mosely for listening to us talk about these stories and giving us your honest feedback. You have been supportive of the dark and Gothic storytelling we wanted to aim for. Thank you for your support and being a good friend to us and a good uncle to our daughter.

Cristina Ortiz and Kaleb Grayson, thank you for your friendship and support.

Thank you to **the Horror Heals Podcast** for having us as guests. We adore you!

Lastly, thank you to all our friends and family.

Notable History & Research

Chapter 1.

Alessandro Volta: inventor of the voltaic pile in 1797, what we have come to know today as the battery.

Cosmic flare: Powerful bursts of energy and radiation that occur from deep space, often associated with astronomical events like supernovae or the activity of black holes and neutron stars. Additionally, Luminous Fast Blue Optical Transients (LFBOTs), which can be billions of times more powerful than the sun. These phenomena are still not fully understood by scientists.

Chapter 2.

The winter of 1816: The winter of 1816 was marked by unusually cold temperatures and severe weather, leading to what is known as the "Year Without a Summer." This was primarily caused by the eruption of Mount Tambora in April 1815, which released ash and gases into the atmosphere, blocking sunlight and resulting in widespread crop failures and food shortages across Europe and North America.

The Italian Tutor Carrack: A carrack is a three- or four-masted ocean-going sailing ship that was developed in the 14th to 15th centuries in Europe. An unidentified Italian or French carrack foundered off Southampton in August or September 1416 while carrying eight hundred troops on board. This ship is noted as having gone missing during its journey.

Brandy in ink: Arctic explorers added alcohol to their ink to lower its freezing point, allowing them to write in extreme cold conditions.

Chapter 3.

The Orange King: Immediately after the collapse of the Empire in the Dutch departments in October 1813, many pamphlets were published describing the atrocities committed by the French. Secondly, and probably more damaging for the Dutch remembrance of Napoleonic rule, was the official policy of forgetting by King William I "THE ORANGE KING" (r. 1813-40). According to this policy of oubli, the Napoleonic period was simply not to be mentioned, whether positively or negatively. Thus, the years 1795-1813 were draped in silence during the Restoration.

The house of Kasper, Jacintha, Laurens, and Augusto:

There were movements of Spanish people to Germany during the 18th century, particularly due to various political and economic factors, including the influence of the Spanish Empire and the interconnectedness of European nations at that time.

C-sections: Ugandans have been practicing cesarean sections since ancient times, with documented evidence of successful procedures occurring in pre-colonial Uganda. A British medical student observed a cesarean section being performed in 1879, indicating that it was a routine and effective practice in the region.

Chapter 5:

The Napoleonic rule: Napoleon Bonaparte established a structured police system in France, known as the "police" or "security state," "De La Police," which was formalized in 1800. This system aimed to maintain public order and ensure the effective implementation of government policies across the country that went relatively unsupervised. Napoleonic rule entered the Dutch Republic in 1795 when the French invaded and established the Batavian Republic, which later transitioned into the Kingdom of Holland in 1806. This period lasted until the Netherlands was fully annexed by the French Empire in 1810. Napoleonic rule effectively ended the Dutch Republic in late November 1813 when the French Empire was defeated, leading to the restoration of Dutch sovereignty. The Netherlands transitioned from being a client state under Napoleon to an independent kingdom, marking a significant shift in its political structure.

The Song of Lord Halewijn: Heer Halewijn is a Dutch folk tale that survives in folk ballad. Although the first printed version of the song only appears in an anthology published in 1848, the ballad itself was first written down in the 13th century but dates back to pre-Christian times and is one of the oldest Dutch folk songs with ancient subject matter to be recorded.

Witch trials: The European witch trials and witch hunts lasted from about (on record) 1450 to 1783. It is estimated that between 40,000 and 60,000 people were executed for witchcraft. Some evidence suggests witch hunts continued into the 1800s due to sporadic trials and executions that occurred in various regions, particularly in Eastern Europe, where beliefs in witchcraft persisted. The last known official witch trial in Poland took place in 1783, indicating that the fear and persecution associated with witchcraft did not completely vanish until later in the 18th century. 100,000 people were prosecuted for witchcraft during the witch trials in Europe and British America, with estimates of 40,000 to 60,000 executions, primarily due to the lack of comprehensive record-keeping and the chaotic nature of the trials. Many accusations and executions went unrecorded, leading to the belief that the actual number of victims could be higher than documented.

Chapter 6

The Lullaby: The song Victoria sings to Susanna is a translation of an extremely old Mesopotamian "lullaby for a newborn." It comes from the library archives at Nineveh (modern-day northern Iraq) and dates to roughly the late 2nd millennium BCE (Middle Babylonian or early Assyrian period). What we know as "The Lullaby" was preserved on a clay tablet in Akkadian (the everyday language of Babylonia and Assyria) and first published by Assyriologists in the early 20th century.

Its extravagant blessings for sturdy growth, plentiful grain, a good wife and son, and protective goddesses, and even the mourning of lizards and flies, mark it as a very ancient mother's song to soothe and ennoble her infant. Scholars don't actually know what the mother herself called this song. No title survives in the Akkadian text. In modern Assyriological publications it's simply referred to as "A Lullaby" (sometimes "The Babylonian Lullaby" or "Akkadian Lullaby"). It can be found in the Assyriological catalogues, and it is usually cited under its museum inventory (publication) number. The most complete copy of this Akkadian lullaby is tablet CBS 12804 in the University of Pennsylvania's Babylonian Section (published in Landsberger's CUSAS 8 edition). You will also occasionally see the same text cross-referenced as K 4447 in the British Museum/Vorderasiatisches Museum Berlin collections.

About the Authors

John Royal Warren is Vienna Nicole's life partner. He is a father first, above all things, and has one previous self-published title, "The Ghosts October Brings." Born in Sioux Falls, South Dakota, he now lives in Arizona. Writing with the belief that "I am creating something I wanted to find in the world. It will be sheer dumb luck if others have been searching for it too."

About Vienna Nicole. In their youth they often spent their time daydreaming, drawing characters, and telling the world they would be an artist someday. They are a mother, raising a brilliant dreamer with their husband, John Royal Warren. This is their debut publication, as they co-author The Dread Legacies series.

• • • •

COMING SOON

THE DREAD LEGACIES

SON OF THE DRAGON

BOOK II

JOHN ROYAL WARREN
&
VIENNA NICOLE

Chapter 1

Son Of The Dragon

The year 2024.

Victoria Frankenstein's red leather-bound journal rests on a black marble desk. Currently, in this room, it is the most alive, in contrast with its otherwise cold surroundings. Two men are seated at the desk with one glaring white light shining down over them. They are dwarfed by the high ceilings in this office. Walls are empty, making it feel more like a box, devoid of windows. An unwelcoming environment where no sense of life has painted the room—no laugh shared—nor idle chit-chat; only calculated orders and business have ever existed in this space. This room feels cold and uninviting, dominated by gloomy shades of grey.

Before the desk sits a man who is nearing 60, though it doesn't appear so, with his physical and mental health flourishing with strong vitality. He is refined with short white hair that is combed to one side and a beard trimmed to his squared-off jaw. His clothes are made for physical practicality in any tactical occasion. He sits without resting against the back of the chair. There is a feature of this man that stands out above all else; carved into the left side of his face is a deep four-claw scar reaching from above his eye to the base of his neck. A souvenir from an incident that occurred so long ago, the scar is a friend that has grown to be a part of him, falling to both sides of his left eye, and luck would have it that his sight was spared in the accident. The markings are spread wide at the top and draw close together at the bottom. The light in the room deepens the shadows of the raised skin of his scars, making their appearance more prominent. When he speaks, his voice is polite with poise, and though abrasive in volume, it is clearly respectful and light, seeming to overcome the gravel that lives there.

"Since procuring the text, it has been verified by our analysts and historians that it is one hundred percent authentic. The signatures and handwriting have been matched to hundreds of other texts, and after the carbon dating authentication protocol, I have reviewed the item. I, myself, have classified it as "Item 1805-1816," in which it refers to the last journal entries of Victoria Lotus Frankenstein. I have added it to the filing of The Frankenstein Journals. To brief you, Victoria begins by writing about the event of 1805 in which an accident occurs—"

"Ezra," the loud and deep voice of the man behind the desk cuts in. Ezra obediently stops talking and adjusts himself to listen. An ancient man is in a dark blue suit, dark the way the void of space is dark, and yet still it retains a blue hue, with a long black coat almost clergyman-like. Dark grey gloves cover his hands, which have metal cuffs on the wrists with the letters "V.H." on them. Thick short strands of his platinum white hair scarcely poke out from under the dark blue homburg hat he is wearing. Large blue eyes with a voided stare sit inside sunken sockets. Rumpled old rubbery skin makes up his emotionless face. He continues while looking at Ezra unblinking, "That is how I understand it. Listen, I am certain I will hear about the contents of this journal with precise analysis. No piece of information in those journals is ever overlooked. Examined to the point of dizzying exhaustion, all secrets squeezed out and fizzed out, without a question of missing any dark corner. I will read every report in its entirety, every single word of the foundation to no end, and I will understand it with its lines of exactitude. What I won't find in those reports is a single opinion. If there is a person of opinion with an exquisite mind in this worldwide organization, I trust that it is with you. Those eyes are never without the turning of gears, and I would rather extract those thoughts than spend a moment with you shilling out more object classifications, security protocols, and procedures. Longitudes & latitudes, proximities, & perimeters. The cold and sharp technical jargon. What are you afraid of, Ezra? What did you find in that journal that is absolutely terrifying?"

Ezra stares back apprehensively, knowing that his viewpoint is going to cause a dangerous reaction in the atmosphere.

"We are harnessing insight... to a kind of creation... that could reshape humankind's entire existence."

Without a motion, the man behind the desk responds, "Now this is worth my energy. Please continue. I would like to hear more on the matter." There is something unsettling about how robotic this man is as he leans forward a few degrees without slouching, yet his ancient withered body remains motionless and stiff, positioned at that angle.

Ezra treats this behavior as a normalcy and continues, "I believe Victoria Frankenstein was two hundred years ahead of her time. She didn't know yet that what she was experimenting with were early forms of genetic engineering. In this journal she explains in great detail what she created. But... what the journal contains more of... is that she unknowingly stumbled through what is essentially the first-ever artificial intelligence. Except for two things. One, there was no trial and error, and two, she perfected it. Erasing the brain's memories and rebooting the human computer to be an immortal battery with one function. It is not bound by the same limitations we are. Imagine a humanoid that does everything better... faster. Faster than any human with a lifetime of experience. It possesses a complex physical ability that lasts longer than that of any human. Impervious to diversions and centered on a single objective with a general knowledge heightened far beyond what any person could ever process."

The man behind the desk sits back. His odd movement becomes

still, with only his eyes traveling in thought, scanning the room from side to side. In a way his movement feels mechanical.

"And are we sure, Ezra? Can we validate that is precisely how it works?"

"We can't know Bartholemew." Ezra drops his head to hear Bartholemew say something that raises indecent tells. In raising his head he continues, "We can't know. We don't even know how it came to work. Neither did Victoria because when she made it, she had no idea what she was even doing. We just know that it works."

Bartholomew moves from one side of his chair to the other and groans in a way that is meant to be a pleased sound, but Ezra can only discern it to be one out of discomfort. "Mmmm," Bartholemew groans again, "Mmmm... Imagine that. If we could copy such an A.I. one million times. It works 24/7, ten times faster. There would be boundless limitations to what could be achieved. Harnessing the discovery of fire."

Ezra's brows crash with a furrow, bowing in the middle as he struggles to keep his composure. Ezra says with a condescending tone, "And I'm sure it goes without mention that whoever controls it holds just as much power."

Bartholomew rotates his head from right to left to put the attention of his eyes on Ezra. "I gather you draw issue from my remarks. Do you perhaps question if my intentions are in opposition to the Van Helsings Foundation?"

Ezra retorts, "I take issue with the idea of replicating—this." He drops his finger onto Victoria's journal. "That in doing so could quite possibly mean replicating it in other human beings. An action that would be immoral. Even if we could, there is no way we can even comprehend its way of thinking. Despite that it's not at the top of my list of concerns, it is worth mentioning that there would be absolutely no way to control it. Let alone millions of copies."

Bartholomew replies, "You talk as though we do not have over a hundred facilities globally with limitless resources. With a few of our great minds, I'm sure we could come to understand it."

Vigorously Ezra shakes his head, "No. That you even entertain the thought is enough to prove how far we are from understanding it. All of humanity as of present, from where Victoria's juggernaut stands, is monumentally far less intelligent, and if you haven't noticed, humans, who are on the top of the food chain, are pretty lacking in empathy for everything... and everyone... that we justify as less intelligent. Pretty violently, I might add."

Bartholomew replies, "Then let's see to it that we remain on the top of the food chain."

One side of a pair of double doors in the office swings open, stirring a cause for interruption. A man in a navy blue wool suit stands with exclamation in the open door. Bartholomew addresses him, "Do you have something to report, director?" The man clasps his hands together and gives Bartholemew and Ezra a nod when saying, "Excuse me, Chairman Bartholemew and Agent Ezra. I have a message for the chairman." He steps in, closing the door behind him, before he says, "It is from Abraham Van Helsing. We have received word that the House Romania field squadron was on the ground in Edinburgh, Scotland. Enabling the procedure code: Last Rights"

A silence settles in the room. Bartholomew stands so quickly his chair falls over. Eyes wide with frustration, he yells at the director, "Abraham is leading the squadron?!"

"No, sir."

"Then who?!"

"Chairman, it is Rada 'Strigoi' Cross."

"With whose approval?!"

Ezra gets up from his seat. "If Strigoi is there, then he could be after Voivode." Ezra comments as he shares a look with Bartholomew.

"Director, what subject are they enabling the procedure code 'Last Rights' on?" Bartholomew questions. The director responds, "The son of the dragon." Bartholomew says, "Code: Last rights requires the approval of every chairman. Strigoi is overstepping. Director, I want you to deploy an advisor squadron to intercept their operation. Get the closest house, the nearest facility, the nearest agent—anyone! Get them to Strigoi's location immediately and allow them to gain control of the operation with the order to rescind the procedure code: last rights. I want Voivode contained. I want Voivode Alive!"

With glossy eyes this man takes another step forward. "With all due respect, Chairman... I am not here to inform you that the squadron is in operation, but that, tragically, 78% of the squadron has been terminated."

The chairman slams his hands on his desk, making a clap, like courtroom gavels, to which silence then follows.

With bulging eyes, the director peers at Bartholomew and continues, "Abraham reports that our records have been falsified. That we do not know the enemy. He described what attacked them as being quadrupedal with phthalo green skin. Brutish nature in its physique. An aggressive, gargantuan, primal, calculated terror. Designed purely to hunt and destroy. Nothing they did... could stop it."

Follow us on:
Bluesky/@thedreadlegacies.bsky.social
instagram/@the_dread_legacies
substacks/@thedreadlegacies
www.thedreadlegacies.weebly.com[1]
Find The Dread Legacies Playlists at Youtube.com and on Spotify.
We are against the use of AI in literature and any media that can be considered an art form. No AI was used, in any of the process, in the making of this book, by the authors or October Leaf Press. All writing, editing, digital art, typography art, cover photography and cover design was all done by
human hands.

www.ingramcontent.com/pod-product-compliance
Lightning Source LLC
Chambersburg PA
CBHW030331030726
47499CB00003B/732